The Old Guard

Tom McKay

MWC Press
Rock Island, Illinois

MWC Press
An imprint of the Midwest Writing Center
401 19th Street
Rock Island, IL
www.mwcqc.org

This book is a work of fiction. Names, characters, places, and incidents are either products of the author's imagination or are used fictionally. Any resemblance to actual events, locales, or persons, living or dead, is coincidental and not intended by the author.

Copyright © 2019 by Thomas R. McKay

First edition: October 2019

Cover design: Ingrid Kallick

ISBN: 978-1-7334802-1-5

ACKNOWLEDGMENTS

A huge thank you is owed to the Midwest Writing Center, ably headed by Ryan Collins. Beyond my gratitude for the publication of *The Old Guard*, I deeply appreciate the many educational opportunities and forums the Center provides to a large and diverse community of writers. Susan Collins served as my liaison with the Center for this project. Sue has helped me at many turns in my adventure as a writer. She and Mary Davidsaver offered thoughtful comments on the manuscript for this novel. Jodie Toohey, president of the Center, donned one of her many hats in the literary world to do the interior design and layout.

The Thursday Morning Writing Group in Madison, Wisconsin continues to offer me the kind of honest critique that every writer needs. Zach Elliot, Ingrid Kallick, Kate McKinney, and Sue Brewster also seemed to laugh in the right places as the group worked through *The Old Guard*. Once again, Ingrid Kallick also provided her creative touch to the cover art.

Tim Fay, publisher and editor of the *Wapsipinicon Almanac*, was kind enough to read the story and offer generous words. Generosity is barely an adequate word to describe the assistance Debbie Kmetz has given me with this and previous books. A writer has to immerse himself in the lives of fictional characters. In real life, my wife, Joyce, cheerfully indulges the time I spend with these imaginary friends. I hope readers will enjoy their time with Patty, Timothy, and the cast of characters in *The Old Guard*.

CHAPTER ONE

Patty jumped up from her kitchen table and high-fived the poster of Danica Patrick taped to the wall. The column Patty had just written for her sports blog, *The Old Guard*, was perfect. Bad professional basketball teams were purposely tanking their seasons. With a bad won/loss record they would get a better position in the NBA draft of college players. To stop tanking, all the league had to do was put the teams that missed the playoffs into a separate single elimination tournament. The team that won the tournament would get the first pick in the draft. A tournament would make all the bad NBA teams try to be as good as possible. This was one of her best ideas ever for *The Old Guard*. She just knew it!

Patty sat back down and stared at her laptop. Now all she needed was a title for her post—something to do with tanks. "Vats Vile: Stop NBA Tanking." "Dear NBA Tankers: No More Tub Flubs." Tub flubs? "No Tanks NBA: Danke Shame." That one didn't really make sense, but with all the foreign players in the league she kind of liked using the German word. It was always the same. The title was the hardest part. She probably needed a break.

Breakfast! It even had break in the word. Perfect! Patty stood and stepped over to the kitchen counter. Actually, a single step did the job in her tiny apartment. She put a piece of Pepperidge Farm thin-sliced white bread into the toaster and positioned a plate nearby. Pouring a bowl of bran flakes and choosing which fruit to put on top came next. She always had dry toast and bran flakes in the morning. A routine was good for a person. She just knew it!

That didn't mean Patty was stuck in a rut. She used different fruits for variety: strawberries, bananas, kiwis, blueberries, cherry tomatoes. Okay, maybe too much variety. Still, tomatoes were a fruit. She shuddered a little at the memory as she pushed down on the toaster and the bread disappeared into the slot.

She slid the plate a little closer to the toaster. Her dad gave her the thing, but it was a fancy one with slots big enough for bagels. Patty never ate bagels. That would throw her day off. She just knew it. It was sweet of her dad to give her the toaster, sort of like the time he gave her the battery-powered tile scrubber. Of course, her bathroom didn't have any tile. She did try it one time when she had an itch she couldn't reach on her back. Funny how long it takes scratches on a person's back to heal.

Same thing with the toaster. Too much power. It was built to pop up bagels. Every morning, it threw her single piece of thin-sliced bread out on the counter. It made her cranky.

That was it! Cranky! The Headline! Patty went right to her laptop and typed in: "Hey NBA! I Get Cranky When You Get Tanky." Perfect! She uploaded her post just as the toaster tossed out her piece of bread. She glanced at the counter. The bread had missed the plate again. She got up, turned to the calendar on the wall, and put an X through another box. Twenty-seven straight days and she still hadn't gotten the toast to land on the plate and stay.

She reached over to the refrigerator and opened the door. Blueberries would be good on her bran flakes today. Before she could grab the clear plastic package, her computer pinged with a message. To heck with the blueberries! She loved getting responses on her blog page. She returned to the screen and read the message. Re: The Old Guard, call ASAP, asap. 1-877-555-2727. Somebody sure was in a hurry and so fast after her post. That tanking column was a good one. She just knew it!

Patty had her smartphone on the table next to the laptop. She entered the number and waited through four rings.

"Good morning. All Sports Athletic Programming, neighbor to The World's Most Famous Arena."

"I had a message to call about *The Old Guard*."

"Old guard?"

"The sports blog."

"One moment please, I'll transfer you to one of our producers."

Patty heard some kind of rustling noise on the other end of the line. That was it! All Sports Athletic Programming. Sports talk radio. She knew about it, but in the Twin Cities, it broadcast out of some kind of low-power FM station on the other side of Minneapolis. It barely came in on her radio. Anyway, she only listened to the major sports networks.

"Fred Frost here. I'm executive producer of the *Fred and Ed Show*. I need to speak to the Old Guard."

"Okay."

"Can you get him?"

"Him?"

"The football player."

"Football?"

"Yeah, football. F-O-O-T-B-A-L-L. Look, lady, I know you're probably not a sports fan. Can you just get the guy?"

"Guy?"

"Yeah, guy. I lost two guests today. I need him on the radio. I like that column on his blog."

"You mean about the tanking?" Patty couldn't believe how fast these guys were.

"Tanking?"

"This morning's post."

"No," Fred said. "The one about the Pro Bowl. About how bad the football was and how to change it like reality TV."

"Oh, right. Football."

"Look, I need the guy. I need to put him on the radio. I told you, I lost two guests today."

"Radio?"

"Yeah, radio. Maybe you've heard of it. You plug it in and push some buttons and noise and shit comes out of it. So is the guy there? This Old Guard?"

"Yes. I mean no . . . I mean not exactly."

"Well, can you exactly get him? I don't have time to dick around."

"Yes, sure. I can definitely get him."

"All right. He's got to call in at 9:35 sharp. This number."

"Right. I've got the number."

"Where the hell is this Old Guard, anyway?"

"Oh, he's not far. I can get him here by 9:35 easy."

"No," Fred said. "I mean where the hell are you? Like we're in New York. You gotta be someplace."

"St. Paul."

"What is that? Minnesota?"

"Right."

"Okay. 8:35 your time. 8:35 sharp."

"Got it."

"Good."

Patty heard the phone click. She put it back on the

table. Her blog on the radio. This wasn't good, it was great. Just one thing. She needed a man!

Meanwhile . . .

Brandon stood over the toilet bowl and unzipped. He looked down and thought his career was probably headed to the same place as the bright blue water. He had graduated from Syracuse University and landed a job at the biggest broadcaster in sports television. Sure, as an assistant producer there he did a lot of grunt work for not much money. Sure, he had kept his eye out for other jobs. Sure, he had only applied for this one on a lark. But now, he worked for a turkey.

When he got the job, moving up so fast to become on-air talent seemed too good to be true. In his case, the old saying should have been reversed, *too true to be good*. All Sports Athletic Programming was neighbor to The World's Most Famous Arena—if you considered fifteen blocks away from Madison Square Garden on a dead-end alley close enough to be called a neighbor. ASAP occupied six tiny rooms and a unisex bathroom along a narrow hallway three flights up from the alley. The "suite" used to be a "massage" parlor. Maybe ASAP had improved the neighborhood. Some days he wondered.

At least the place had a clean bathroom. Tiffany kept on everybody about that. Of course, her job at the reception desk was about three feet from the bathroom door. She was obsessed with having a fresh cake of bowl cleaner clipped under the rim of the toilet at all times. That, and never being called Tiff. Maybe it was hard being a 55-year-old woman named Tiffany.

It definitely was hard working for Fred Frost. The moment Brandon signed his contract, Fred informed him his name wouldn't be Brandon Edwards anymore. On air he was Ed Brandon. In fact, Fred told Brandon he was only hired because it was easy to switch his first and last names. The *Fred and Ed Show* had a nice ring to it.

Brandon took aim at the blue cake of bowl cleaner and made a direct hit. Clearly it was a case of the aim being better than the goal. Brandon's shoulders sagged. He recognized a metaphor for his career when he saw one.

He knew he should hurry. He couldn't be late getting back in the studio. The commercial break was only three-and-a-half minutes long. Fred wouldn't be back at the microphone in time. He was on the phone. Brandon did all the booking, but both call-in guests this morning cancelled. Talk about somebody being pissed, Fred was so mad that he said he would make the call himself to that blogger, the Old Guard.

That was a joke. One guest got sick, but Fred messed up the other one on his own. Sure, Jack Williams was a backup quarterback in the Arena League, but he was married to a swimsuit model. At least some people had heard of her. ASAP didn't get much closer than that to big names in sports.

Unfortunately, when Brandon forwarded Fred the email from Jack Williams confirming his appearance, Fred replied, "The only thing interesting about that guy is his wife's ass." Apparently, Fred still had trouble understanding what clicking on "reply all" meant. That was the end of Jack Williams as a guest.

Life as the neighbor of The World's Most Famous Arena wasn't easy. Brandon sighed and flushed the toilet. Before he could even zip up, he heard Tiffany's voice, "Ed, put down that toilet seat."

Mean, meanwhile . . .

Timothy sat on a stool at the breakfast island in his apartment with his head bent over a slow-cooker full of steaming water. Even though he was single, he was glad he had rented a two-bedroom apartment when he moved in two weeks ago. He had looked first at a one-bedroom unit one floor up on the other side of the hallway. It was tiny. The itty-bitty kitchen didn't have a nice spot like this to set up his great-grandmother's remedy for a head cold.

He didn't do it exactly his great-grandmother's way. She put some kind of menthol rub in the water and then heated it to boiling before taking it off the stove. Timothy had the advantage there. The slow-cooker made a lovely even heat. The bath towel he draped over his head did the job to hold the steam in, but it didn't compare to his great-grandmother's delightful tea towels. Each one was embroidered with a day of the week. After all these years, he still remembered that she gave him the Tuesday towel because that was the day he got sick when he was visiting her.

It was funny how memories worked. He had perfect recall of the lavender embroidery on the tea towel, but he couldn't remember how she got the greasy menthol rub to mix with the water. Maybe the heat just melted it in. It didn't much matter since he didn't have any menthol rub. He used some peppermint extract that he brought home from the pastry shop. He inhaled as deeply as his stuffed-up nose allowed. The peppermint seemed to be working.

On a normal morning, he'd be well into his day at work. Right about now, he would be taking the last croissants out of the oven, putting the cream puffs he had filled into the bakery case, and snitching a butter cookie or two. He patted his belly. Maybe he snitched too many butter cookies. He breathed in again. He knew he shouldn't mope about a little old cold. He loved his life owning a pastry shop. He started a rhyme to himself. Hey Dope – Don't Mope – Have Hope. He liked his new little saying. It could make a nice cross-stitch to hang somewhere.

Suddenly, someone pounding on his front door

obliterated his thoughts of cross-stitch. Before he could move, it happened again accentuating the pounding in his sinuses. He didn't need Hey Dope on a cross-stitch. There was a real dope at his front door.

"Coming," Timothy called back at another barrage of pounding. He clutched the bath towel in his hand and walked to the apartment door. He opened it to see a short woman in a Minnesota Vikings sweatshirt looking up at him.

"I need help," she said. "I have an emergency."

Timothy dropped the towel. "Oh, dear. Should I call 911? I'll get my phone."

"Not that kind of emergency. I need a man."

"Oh, well—"

"I can't wait!"

"Dear me, I'm not sure I'm suitable for your needs."

"Needs?"

"Well . . ."

"No, not that kind of man. I'm the Old Guard."

"Pardon?"

"I'm the Old Guard, but they think I'm a man."

Timothy looked down at her cute nose and pert eyes. Mistaken identity seemed highly unlikely although her short brown hair could have used a little styling.

"I write a blog. It's called *The Old Guard*. They want me on the radio."

"Radio?"

"Sports radio. I write a sports blog."

"Oh."

"The blog is named *The Old Guard* because I used to be a guard in high school."

"What did you guard?"

"Basketball!"

"You guarded basketballs?"

"I played basketball. I was a guard because I was short." Her coach always said she was short and spunky.

She liked being called spunky.

"Wouldn't tall people be better for guarding?"

"No! Okay, sometimes. I mean, well, never mind about that."

"Right."

"Here's the thing. They think I'm a man because I wrote about the Pro Bowl."

"Pro Bowl?"

"Pro Bowl. Football. You do know what football is, right?"

"Oh my, yes. It's on TV on Sundays. Right before my favorite show about the woman who serves as Secretary of State. If the football isn't over in time, it's still going when I turn on the television."

"Great," Patty sighed.

"I know," Timothy said, "it's so disappointing when that happens."

"Sure. Right. Anyway, back to football. I wrote about football, so they think I'm a football player. Guards play on the line."

"Are those the really big guys who line up across from each other?"

"Yes!" There could be a glimmer of hope for this guy. She just knew it!

"I bet that's why they call it the line. Of course, the way they run into each other, you'd think they would call it attacking rather than guarding."

There was no hope for this guy. She just knew it.

Timothy leaned against the door frame. "I suppose I should watch more football if I want to understand."

"Do you know anything about sports?" Patty asked.

"I used to play a pretty mean game of croquet at my great-grandmother's house. Of course, I was just little then."

"Well, you're not little now."

"I know. I've always been tall . . . and a little

overweight."

"Sorry. I didn't mean anything. I just need help." She tugged on Timothy's arm. "My apartment is right across the hall."

"I'm sure it's cozy."

"No, you have to come." She tugged on his arm again. "This is my one chance on the radio."

"Come along so you can go on the radio?"

"No, you."

"Me?"

"What have I been saying?"

"They think the Old Guard is a man."

"Bingo."

"So, I have to be you on the radio?"

"Double bingo!"

"I hate to bring it up, but my voice doesn't sound anything like yours."

"Ugh."

"Oh, right. The Old Guard is a man even if she's really a woman. I mean if you are. Well, of course, you are."

"Look, please, we haven't got much time. Can you help?"

"Well, I do like to be a good neighbor."

CHAPTER TWO

Timothy followed his neighbor across the hall. She turned as she opened the door to her apartment. "My name's Patty, by the way."

"I'm Timothy." He paused inside the door to glance at the big-screen TV, aluminum chaise lounge lawn chair with green and white nylon straps, floor lamp, and metal folding chair that furnished the living room. "I think the minimalist look can be quite bold."

"It's just old stuff I got out of the rafters in my dad's garage."

"Oh, yes, of course, I should have said retro."

"Whatever. Come in the kitchen. We haven't got much time."

"For what?" he asked.

"To get you ready."

"They won't see me on radio."

"Not that kind of ready. You have to read my post so you understand. You're on in twenty minutes."

"By myself?"

"They're going to interview you. You answer their questions about my Pro Bowl post."

"What's a pro bowl?"

"Football. It's an all-star game, and it's lousy."

"Aren't All-Stars supposed to be good?"

"My point, exactly. They don't try hard."

"That's not very sporting."

"They don't want to get hurt in an exhibition." Patty pulled out the chair at her kitchen table where the laptop waited. "Here, sit down and read the post. The idea is to change the Pro Bowl to competitions like reality TV. It's satirical."

"This is getting complicated."

"Just read. You'll catch on." Patty watched Timothy's eyes scan the screen. A smile began to form at the corners of his mouth. Even he was getting it. That had to mean it was good. She just knew it!

"This is very droll," Timothy said. "Oh, here's the TV dance shows. I do like to watch those. Don't you just love the costumes? Hmm. Well, I don't know that the idea of two men dancing together has to be funny."

"Come on! It's the quarterback and a defensive end doing the tango. What lineman doesn't want to throw around a quarterback?"

"Don't they guard them? I thought you said linemen are guards."

Patty bopped the heel of her hand against her forehead. "The guards are offensive lineman."

"Oh." Timothy sniffled.

"Are you okay?"

"I've got a little cold."

"I thought you sounded kind of nasal." Patty rummaged around in her junk drawer for a bottle then drew a glass of water at the sink. "Here take this."

"What is it?"

"Cold medicine. Fast acting."

"Oh, my, I'm a little sensitive to medicines."

"Please, just take it. They're mild." Patty had no idea what kind of cold medicine it was. She only used herbal remedies. This bottle was something her dad had given her. "We can't have your nose running in the middle of the interview."

"Well, if you say so." Timothy swallowed the pill.

"God, look at the time. We have to call!"

This would never work. She just knew it.

"I haven't finished reading."

Patty picked up her smartphone and redialed the ASAP number. "I'll stand over by the radio and give signals."

"About what?"

"To help."

"How?"

Patty had no idea how, but a voice on the phone saved her from having to make something up. "This is All Sports Athletic Programming, neighbor to The World's Most Famous Arena."

"Hi, my name is Patty. I have the Old Guard on the line for the *Fred and Ed Show*."

"Have him hold. I'll put him through in 45 seconds."

Patty heard the audio from the show come through the phone. They were in a commercial. She closed her laptop and handed Timothy the phone. "You're on in 45 seconds."

"Oh, my."

"I'll be right over at my radio," she said.

"Oh, dear."

Patty moved down to the end of the kitchen counter, put in earbuds, and turned on her portable radio. It was one her dad bought her with a cassette tape player built in. She didn't have any cassette tapes or any idea where her dad found the radio. It must have been a closeout.

She looked over at Timothy and saw beads of sweat

forming on his forehead. She kept tapping the tuning button as she scrolled down the FM band. Finally, she landed on 94.4. All Sports Athletic Programming barely came in. She thought she heard a commercial still playing. She adjusted the antenna and the sound cleared up. As soon as she took her hand away, the signal faded. She touched the antenna again. Sound! She let loose. No sound!

She took hold of the antenna once more just in time to hear, "Welcome back sports friends, fans, and full-blown fanatics. This is the *Fred and Ed Show* on the ASAP network. I'm Fred Frost."

"And I'm Ed Brandon."

"Our first guest is joining us, as always, on the ASAP morning hotline sponsored by Upstate Maple Syrup, The Slowest Syrup in the East."

"I had some on my pancakes this morning," Ed said.

"Thank you, Ed. No wonder you barely made it to the studio on time. We'll have to see if our guest did the same. He is the Old Guard who blogs about a variety of sports topics. Welcome to the *Fred and Ed Show*."

Patty looked over at Timothy who didn't answer. He had frozen up already.

Timothy gave her a weak smile then she heard his voice through the radio, "Thank you." She slapped her forehead as she realized the show had a built-in audio delay. The signal faded out until she put her hand back on the antenna.

". . . understand you love football and are pretty upset with the quality of play," Ed said.

"That's right," Timothy answered.

Fred cut in, "Well, you've got some pretty creative ideas on how to liven things up."

"That's right."

"The play in the Pro Bowl is worse every year, with no one wanting to get hurt in what is essentially an exhibition game," Ed said.

"That's right."

Patty rolled her eyes. Maybe Timothy wouldn't ever say anything more than "that's right." She took her free hand and flapped her fingers together in a talking motion.

"So, first things first, should we call you Old or Guard?" Fred laughed.

"Either one," Timothy said.

"I guess it's take our pick. How about I call you Old and Ed calls you Guard." Fred practically chortled.

Patty didn't hear anything from Ed. Maybe he didn't think Fred's line was any more chortleworthy than she did.

"So okay, Old, you were a football player?"

"That's right."

"Where?"

"High school."

"I think what my colleague means, Mr. Guard, is what town?"

"Oh, dear. Right . . . town . . . of course . . . Rockdale."

"You had me worried there, Old. For a minute, I thought you had one too many hits to the head and forgot."

"That would be Rockdale, Minnesota?" Ed asked.

"Minnesota, oh dear. No. Kansas."

"Kansas?"

"That's right. The Rockdale Rockets. Rah! Rah! Rockets! Shoot the Moon!"

"Shoot the Moon?" Ed said.

"Our cheer. You know, for rockets."

"Makes sense, Ed." Fred had his chortle going again. "With the Old Guard and his fellow linemen all bent over, I'll bet there were plenty of moons being shot."

Patty turned her back to Timothy and flipped the bird to the radio.

"Anyway, why don't we get back to your thoughts

about the Pro Bowl," Ed said.

"Right," Fred cut in, "you think that the game is so lousy that it should be replaced by football players in skills competitions."

"That's right."

"But not football skills," Fred cut in again. "Instead, skills from reality TV."

"You came up with some doozies," Ed said. "A tailgating cook-off called 'The Sheet Metal Chef.'"

"Well, of course, that was Patty's idea," Timothy said.

Patty let go of the antenna. She waved her arms and shook her head.

"Who's Patty?" Fred asked.

"Uh, Patty, uh . . . Cakes."

"You have a partner called Patty Cakes," Fred said. "Sounds like another big ol' lineman who could shoot a good moon."

"Oh, no, she's uh, uh, my associate. Of course, Patty Cakes is her nickname. She helps, but, but, I'm the real Old Guard. And, of course, I do love the all chef's competitions on TV. I probably should have added a baking component to my column. Petit fours, I think."

"Petit fours," Ed said. "You think those are too tough for Pro Bowlers to tackle?"

"Tackle?" Timothy said. "Oh, right, tackle, that's from football. My goodness, yes, petit fours would be very amusing. The icing is so difficult for big fat fingers. I know that I struggle with them."

"So wait, Old, you're telling me that you bake little cakes?"

"I'm a pastry chef. I went to culinary school."

"Not a regular college?" Ed asked. "Didn't you want to play football?"

"Oh, no," Timothy blurted. "All that rolling around in the dirt."

"Ah ha," Fred snickered. "One of those guys who likes

watching it more than doing it."

Patty flipped the bird at the radio again.

"Whattaya say we move on, Fred. Mr. Guard included dancing as a good reality TV competition for the Pro Bowl players."

"I see that, Ed. Old, here, makes a good point about the tango. Those defensive lineman could really get into throwing around quarterbacks."

"And he's right about the minuet," Ed said. "That would be a perfect fit for the Patriots."

Timothy spoke up, "Now, I really wouldn't call the minuet a patriotic dance. I believe it was favored more by the British aristocracy than the American colonists."

Patty shuddered. Timothy had no idea that the Patriots were a football team. She tried to mouth the words "football team" and understood the look of panic on his face when she heard Fred say on the delay, "Hey, Old, the minuet was your idea, not mine."

Patty had to signal Timothy. There was a marker on the counter but no paper. She had stolen a couple of her dad's t-shirts that she kept in the broom closet for dust rags. They were white. Maybe she could write on one of them.

Just as Patty was about to take her hand from the antenna and open the closet door, she heard Fred ask, "So, Old, did you have any other ideas for reality TV takeoffs that you didn't put in your column?"

Patty thought of singing. They could have players do the National Anthem. That was part of every football game. Maybe she could write that on a t-shirt, but she didn't want the radio to fade out.

"Well, yes, ideas," Timothy said. "They do come and go, don't they?"

Patty kicked off one of her flip flops, and it flew toward Timothy's head.

He ducked just in time. "Kicking could be one."

"Of course, that's already part of football," Ed said.

"Yes . . . no . . . right. The foot part." Timothy looked over at Patty standing on one foot with the toes of her other foot curled around the antenna as she pulled a t-shirt out of the broom closet. "Perhaps a wet t-shirt contest."

"For football players?" Ed said.

"I don't know. Maybe Old, here, is on to something," Fred chimed in. "Some of those football players have pretty big pecs."

Timothy kept his eyes on Patty as she shook her head and struggled to keep her balance.

"Yoga," he said. "Some of those poses are very hard to strike."

"Well, that's all the time we have for our pastry baking, yoga posing—" were the last words Patty heard Fred say before she fell to the floor with her earbuds pulling the radio along. The electrical cord ripped out of the socket, tangled with the bagel toaster, and brought both appliances crashing to the floor. The sound of crashing appliances in the background was not the best way to end a radio interview. She just knew it.

CHAPTER THREE

Patty didn't even have her earbuds out before Timothy jumped up from his chair at the table.

"Oh heavens, let me hel—" He never finished the sentence as he crashed to the floor.

Patty twirled her leg and tried to untangle the radio cord that wrapped around her ankle. Sure, she had needed a man, but not a dead one on her kitchen floor. She rolled across the patterned vinyl, dragging the radio behind her, and put her head on his chest. His heart was beating. He actually smelled kind of good. It had to be some kind of cologne. Who puts on cologne to stay home with a cold? It was cologne, not deodorant. She just knew it!

At his apartment, Timothy had offered to call 911 for her. Maybe she needed to do that now for him. She scooted up close to his ear and whispered, "Timothy, can you hear me?"

"Quite clearly." His eyelids fluttered and he lifted his head. "Do you know you have a radio tied to your leg?"

"Yes . . . I mean, no . . . I mean, the cord is just

tangled."

"It's going to be awfully uncomfortable walking around that way."

"What?"

"Just a joke," he said.

"Maybe my kitchen floor isn't the best place for a comedy routine."

"Oh." Timothy gently patted the floor. "Sorry."

"That's okay. I just meant maybe we should get up." Patty reached down and freed her ankle from the electrical cord.

Timothy rolled over and got to his knees. "Oh my, I'm still a little woozy."

Patty stood beside him and clutched his arm. "Can you make it to the chair? I'll help."

"Okay." He straightened up slowly as Patty tugged on his arm. He wobbled a little then plopped down on the chair.

"You made it." At the moment, she was glad she had purchased the small oak dinette set at a yard sale. With the wings down, it didn't take up much room in her little kitchen, and the chairs were really sturdy. A guy Timothy's size plopping down on one of them put the chair to the test. This dinette set would really last. She just knew it!

Timothy rubbed his eyes.

"Are you okay?" Patty asked.

"I'm still a little light-headed. It might be the medicine on an empty stomach."

"You haven't eaten anything?" She glanced at the warnings on the medicine bottle: One pill every eight hours . . . dizziness . . . don't drink alcohol . . . take with food . . . stop taking and call your doctor. The only thing the stuff didn't warn about was an erection lasting more than four hours.

". . . clear my head. Normally, I would have been at

work for hours by now."

"Pardon?" she asked as she tuned back into the conversation. "You would have been at work for hours?"

"The life of a pastry chef. Bake before dawn while the rest of the world sleeps."

"Oh, right. Pastry chef. You said that on the radio." Patty wished she didn't remember that or anything else about the interview. "Maybe you need something to eat. I can make some toast."

"That might help."

She took her loaf of thin-sliced bread out of the refrigerator. "One piece or two?"

"Won't you join me? I wouldn't feel right eating in front of you."

Patty didn't want any more toast. She already had her one slice for the day. Still, she'd almost killed the guy with cold medicine. "Sure, I'll have a piece. You want something to drink? Milk? Juice?"

"A cup of black tea would be lovely."

Patty drank tea. Herbal tea. She had peppermint, lemongrass, chamomile, and six other kinds. Then, she remembered the box of Lipton's her dad gave her one time. She dragged one of the heavy oak chairs over to the counter and stood on it to reach the tea on the top shelf of the upper cabinet.

"Can I help?"

"You just sit still." She hopped down from the chair with the box in her hand. Patty turned on the burner under the tea kettle, sent two slices of bread into the toaster, and placed two plates next to it. At least now, she had two chances to catch a flying piece of toast. She'd get one this time. She just knew it! While the water heated and the toast toasted, she turned to the refrigerator and took out a tub of margarine.

"Are you sure I can't help?"

"No, you've done enough already."

"The interview," he said, "tell me the truth. Was that a disaster?"

Meanwhile . . .

Fred yanked off his headphones and spit out, "That was a disaster," as a commercial for Upstate Maple Syrup played on air.

"I know," Ed answered.

"It doesn't do any good to know now. We got the slowest syrup in the East for a sponsor, and you find us the slowest dimwit in Kansas for a guest."

"Minnesota."

"What?"

"Minnesota," Ed said. "He lives in Minnesota now."

"Who the hell cares?" Fred threw down his headset. "You can take the next segment on your own. You try to figure out something to say after that shit."

Fred stormed out of the studio, grabbed the newspaper off of Tiffany's desk, and went into the bathroom. She stared after him as she heard Ed say on the radio, "Welcome back, and welcome is the word. We welcome your opinions on what our last guest had to say about the Pro Bowl. And, of course, your comments on any other topics are also welcome. We are the All Sports Athletic Programming network and, as we like to say, neighbors to The World's Most Famous Arena."

While Ed tap-danced on the air, the phone rang at Tiffany's desk. She answered as always with "All Sports Athletic Programming, neighbor to The World's Most Famous Arena."

"Hi, I'm a caller. That's why I'm calling in. You want callers, right? You put callers on the show?"

"Fred and Ed always welcome callers." Technically, Tiffany knew this was true although they almost never had any. "What are you calling about?"

"I want to talk about that Old Guard guy. He was okay, so, you know, I called."

"Please hold sir and I'll put you through to Fred and Ed." She realized that was going to be some trick with Fred in the bathroom. Tiffany opened the line to Ed's headset. "I have a caller I'm putting through. He wants to talk about the Old Guard."

"And I understand we have a caller on the Upstate Maple Syrup hotline," Ed said on air. "Remember, Upstate Maple Syrup is the slowest syrup in the East. Go ahead, sir."

"Yes?"

"Go ahead."

"Am I on?"

"You're on the Upstate Maple Syrup hotline."

"I am? I'm a caller. I wanted the radio show."

"And this is the *Fred and Ed Show*. Do you have a comment?"

"It's that Old Guard."

"Right. Our guest this morning."

"Yeah, that's why I'm calling. He's all right by me. That's what I wanted to say."

"Okay. There you have it. A fan of the Old Guard. We always love to hear from our audience."

Tiffany spoke into Ed's headset. "Another caller."

"Looks like we have another caller," Ed said. "You're on ASAP."

"Yeah, that last guy is nuts. That Old Guard stinks."

"Well, you certainly have your opinion."

"That's right. Let me tell you. Making fun of football. Complaining about rolling around in the dirt. Dirt is what's great about America."

"How's that?" Ed asked.

"Dirt. You're always hearing about the great things that happen on American soil."

"Yes?"

"Soil's dirt."

"So it is."

"That's all I got to say."

Tiffany's phone rang again. She sent the call through as she stretched out the phone cord far enough to knock on the bathroom door. "Fred, you gotta get out here. You're getting calls."

". . . so you agree with the Old Guard?" Ed said.

"I do. The Pro Bowl is lousy every year. Some of the ideas that guy said were really funny. Like the yogurt."

Ed cut in, "I believe it was yoga."

"No, I'm sure it was yogurt. He was talking about cooking contests. Yogurt's food."

"So it is," Ed sighed.

"Anyway, you should get the Old Guard on again."

"Thanks for your comments. Looks like the Upstate Maple Syrup hotline is still lit up. Let's hear from our next caller. Go ahead, please."

"Yeah, I called about the first moron, but that last moron was just as bad. Get rid of that Old Guard. Yoga, yogurt it's all a bunch of liberal shit."

Ed cut off the caller. "There's another opinion. I'm waiting for more."

Wait he did as he let five seconds of dead air pass while he listened during the delay and bleeped out the word *shit*. He caught it just as Fred was coming back into the studio. Where the hell had he been? Operating the dump button was most of the reason they had to have two people in the studio. Ed could bleep something out if he had to while Fred kept on talking.

"Fred, we have quite a controversy here about the Old Guard," Ed said on air.

"Yes we do," Fred answered as if he had any idea what was going on.

"Maybe we should make that our Barnaby's Fishing Rods poll question. Should we have the Old Guard back as a guest?"

"I know how I'm voting," Fred said.

"Just so our listeners understand, only their votes count. Go to the ASAP website before tomorrow's show and vote on the Barnaby's Fishing Rods poll question. Should we have the Old Guard back? Yes or no?"

"I guess that about wraps it up for today's *Fred and Ed Show*," Fred said as he glanced down at the sheet Ed handed him. "Stay tuned for the *Internet Scorebook* next on ASAP. Then, get all of your major league baseball spring training news with the *Arizona Journal* at ten-thirty, followed by the *Florida Report* at eleven. And don't forget to listen at eight o'clock tonight for *Sports of Every Sort* with Wayne Bender. This evening Wayne is in Shrewsbury, New Jersey for the International Hamster Racing Championships."

Mean, Meanwhile . . .

Patty stood by the toaster as two slices of bread popped up then settled back down into their slots. That was great. All she had to do was make toast for two people every morning and her toaster would be fine. She buttered one piece and put it on a plate for Timothy who had daintily removed the tea bag from his cup.

He finished a sip of tea and said, "Thank you."

"No problem. Go ahead and eat. I'll butter mine."

He did as instructed while Patty finished at the counter and moved to the table.

"Is it okay?" she asked.

"Delightful."

"Good."

Timothy took another bite of his toast. He chewed politely and swallowed. "You had the perfect idea. I do believe a little food is helping. I always think this brand is a lovely commercial bread."

"I'm glad you feel better."

"I hope you feel a little better, too. I know the interview got off to a bad start."

Patty fought the urge to say *that's right*.

"I thought I recovered somewhat on the dancing. I'm sure I was right about the minuet."

"Timothy, the Patriots are a football team."

"Oh, dear."

"They're like the most famous team there is."

"I thought that was the Cowboys or something." Timothy took a sip of tea.

"They're famous, too, but not as good."

"Well, I imagine it was the name Cowboys that caught my fancy."

Patty pushed aside her half-eaten piece of toast. "Yeah, about names, you made up a whole town in Kansas. Why did you say Rockdale?"

"It just came to me. I thought I had to say something. I've always wanted to visit Kansas. I just think about the amber waves of grain." He started to sing, "Oh, beautiful for spacious skies—"

"I get it. I get it. But you still made up a town."

"Well, gracious sakes, Patty, you made up a whole person."

"Huh?"

"Me."

Patty threw her arms up. "It's not the same thing. You're a real person, and the Old Guard is a real person."

"So, I impersonated him. Or is it her?" Timothy chuckled. "That will tickle Martin pink. Me a female impersonator."

Patty put her head between her hands.

"It is kind of funny," Timothy said.

She glanced up. "Who's Martin?"

"Oh, my partner. We met in culinary school. We've had the bakery for six years."

"You've been together for six years?"

"I feel we've established a very good business. I refer to it as a bakery, but it's really just a sweet shop. Cookies, cakes, pastries, and the like."

"What's it called?"

"The Sweet Shoppe."

"Oh."

"Not very creative, I guess."

It wasn't very creative, but Patty could help with that. She just knew it! "I have my own business. I design logos and letterhead."

"My, my, how interesting."

"Here, I'll show you." She dragged her heavy oak chair around the table and slid it next to Timothy's so they could both look at her laptop. "I have a website."

"Good marketing, I'm sure."

"Right, right. I work from home, right here on my computer."

"Isn't it an amazing world. I hope computers don't make pastry chefs obsolete someday."

"Here. Here it is. See?"

Timothy stared at the fancy script on the screen. "Logo Toga?"

"No! LoGo ToGo. It's the name of the business. That's an O."

"Oh, dear me, yes it is. I'm afraid I'm not very visual. Down at the bakery, Martin has to decorate all the birthday cakes and frost the smiley-face cookies and the like."

"Here, let me show you one I did for a lady who crochets dog toys. She calls her business Pooch Palz." Patty's fingers tapped away at the keyboard until the Pooch Palz logo came up.

Timothy clucked his tongue. "Well, look at that. The words pooch and palz share that one tall P, and there are little doggie faces in the Os."

"The woman really liked it," Patty said.

"My, isn't that 'z' instead of an 's' on Palz clever."

"I thought that up. The woman liked that, too."

"Heavens, I should think so. Did you draw the little doggies?"

"No, I took them off the Internet. They're like clip art. I have a subscription."

"Ah, overhead. Just like the bakery. We have our costs nobody sees."

"My designs are real economical for people. Like, I do a lot of work for small non-profits. I just finished a letterhead for the New Age Historical Society."

"You don't say."

"Yeah, that New Age stuff's been around longer than you think. The society is like a bunch of old Baby Boomers."

"Think." Timothy tapped his temple.

"What?"

"You just said the word think." He pointed at the computer. "We didn't think to check Rockdale, Kansas on the Internet. What if there is one?"

"Right, and Santa Claus and the Easter Bunny live there."

"My great-grandmother always told me that Santa lives at the North Pole." Timothy winked. "I don't believe she ever mentioned the Bunny's residence."

Patty rolled her eyes and started tapping the computer keys again.

Timothy practically jumped out of his chair when an image flashed on the screen. "Look, a picture."

They both stared silently at the caption below: Fortieth reunion of the last graduating class of Rockdale High School. Rah! Rah! Rockets!

CHAPTER FOUR

"Worms," Patty muttered. She looked down at her phone and thought that WORM just about topped off the morning. For starters, when she made breakfast, her toast missed the plate again. She couldn't bear listening to sports talk radio after yesterday's disaster, not that she listened to ASAP, anyway. The thing was, she couldn't even turn on her favorite program on the good sports network.

Why did the Warming Oppression Resistance Movement have to find her today, or ever find her at all? This was the first time since she started LoGo ToGo that she had turned down work. She tried to be nice about it. She told them a logo based on a worm might not be very inspiring, maybe even having WORM as an acronym wasn't the best idea.

The WORM people had their own ideas. Since they had her on a speaker phone, she had to listen to those ideas coming from five or six different voices. No way could she keep them all straight. They had chosen a name with the WORM acronym on purpose, and they wanted a worm logo—a snarling worm to show that the worm had turned. They weren't going to stand for the global warming hoax anymore. Everybody knew it was a plot from a bunch of scientists at universities full of liberals.

One guy wanted the snarling worm rearing up on its back legs. When Patty pointed out that worms don't have legs, another guy said to make the worm all coiled up and ready to strike "like one of them big python snakes." Patty figured he meant a king cobra. Maybe the guy needed some scientist from one of those universities full of liberals to teach him the difference. Patty cut the conversation short. There was no way she was going to take a job from a bunch of nitwits who thought global warming was a hoax.

She didn't mind turning down the money. It wasn't like she was going to make a fortune working for WORM. Actually, she didn't care much about a fortune, but a little bit of fame for her blog would have been all right. She didn't see that chance coming again. Not with Timothy doing radio interviews for her. He was nice and all, but he didn't know anything about sports. *The Old Guard* was done for on the radio. She just knew it.

Meanwhile . . .

"Clams," Fred muttered. He had just closed the *Fred and Ed Show* with the usual promo for Wayne Bender's *Sports of Every Sort*. Tonight, Wayne was going to be in Bivalve, New Jersey for the International Clamshell Skipping Championships.

"You say something?" Ed asked.

"I said clams. Who the hell gives a rip about clamshells? The only way I would listen to this shit Wayne Bender puts on the air is if I was on a bender myself. To hell with it. I'm going to the reading room."

Fred stormed out before Ed had a chance to say anything. Not that Ed wanted to talk to Fred, anyway. Three hours on air with Fred was more than enough of that. Of course, Ed could have pointed out that Wayne Bender owned All Sports Athletic Programming. It was Wayne who poured enough money into the operation to keep the network afloat and Fred and Ed employed. Wayne could do whatever program he wanted about hamsters, clams, or any other animal in the world of sports.

Ed pulled out the scripts he wrote yesterday for the *Arizona Journal* and *Florida Report* spring training shows. It was simple enough. The programs were just clips from local radio stations in major league cities that sent baseball reporters to cover spring training. Ed pieced together downloads from satellite radio and interjected his own scintillating copy such as, "Now, here's former major league relief pitcher Stony Stonewall reporting from Philadelphia Phillies' camp in Clearwater, Florida."

On ASAP, yesterday's baseball news followed the latest sports scores on the *Internet Scorebook* with Fred Frost. For a guy who couldn't even use email right, Fred thought he was some kind of Internet genius. He spent his program jumping from website to website for the major sports leagues and reading the scores. He loved his tag line, "The Internet Scorebook, The Only Sports Program in Cyber Speed." It never seemed to occur to him that on a show airing at eleven in the morning, all the scores were from the previous evening and just about everybody could go on the Internet to find results on their own for the teams they followed. Listening to Fred drone through a whole screen of scores was the last thing anyone needed to do.

Right now, Ed needed to figure out the computer glitch that had kept him from tabulating the Barnaby's Fishing Rods poll question responses for the morning's show. If he got lucky recovering the poll results, he might have time to click around the Internet for any new job possibilities.

Mean, Meanwhile . . .

"Ants," Timothy muttered. He needed something to cheer himself up. He could make some ants-on-a-log for lunch like his great-grandmother did when he was a little boy. They always seemed like such a treat. Martin had made him some delicious chicken soup which would be just the thing for Timothy's cold. He felt better today, but not well enough to go to the bakery. A pastry chef who was under the weather couldn't handle food for the public. That was a no-no. Still, he hated missing work. That really was the worst. He missed making sweet treats to bring a little happiness into the world, and, of course, he missed Martin.

Skipping work yesterday hadn't been so bad. Not that he wasn't sicker yesterday, but the morning turned out to be quite an adventure. That Patty was really something. The whole episode certainly lifted him out of his doldrums with the possible exceptions of the part where he got stuck saying "that's right," or the fact that he didn't know the Patriots were a football team, or the moment he passed out on the kitchen floor.

Still, he did find her company much more stimulating than being stuck at home alone with a cold. He certainly enjoyed the cup of tea and the lovely little slice of bread Patty toasted for him. He had to bring a loaf of that brand home from the market someday soon.

Mean, Mean, Meanwhile . . .

"Rats," Ed muttered. He'd finally solved the problem with the poll question just as Fred opened the studio door.

That meant no time for checking the job boards. Even so, he could feel a faint smile forming on his lips. "Fred, I got the results of the poll question pulled up."

"A little late, don't you think?"

"Do you want to hear them?"

"What," Fred said, "that people think some guy who calls himself the Old Guard is a dip-shit?"

"It's a four-to-one ratio," Ed answered. "The listeners want him back."

CHAPTER FIVE

Who stops and thinks anymore? Patty wondered if anybody did. Like the word *gherkin*. It was a funny word. That made her curious where the word came from. She had never heard anyone talk about it. Gherkins weren't hiding. They were in stores and kitchen cabinets and refrigerators all over the place, and still nobody asked where the word came from. Because people don't stop and think.

She had the gherkins out to make tuna salad. Maybe everything had gone wrong with Timothy and ASAP Radio, but at least she learned one thing—she could outsmart her toaster with two slices of bread. She still hadn't caught a single slice popping onto her plate at breakfast, but for lunch, tuna salad was a great strategy. She'd toast two slices of bread for her sandwich. That would keep it in the slots. She could beat a toaster. She just knew it!

Patty still wondered about the word *gherkin*. A good tuna salad really needed gherkins. She reached into a bottom drawer of her cabinets for the copy of *Who Knew? Facts Fit for Fun*. Her dad gave it to her two years ago. She never really found anything in it, but maybe it had something about gherkins. She laid the heavy tome on the table and thumbed through the Gs. No gherkins. She looked down at the empty bottom drawer where she kept the book. Most people probably used that drawer to store pans. Patty didn't have many pans. She put the book back in place and closed the drawer. Patty wondered if she would be better off getting more pans.

Wikipedia was the place where Patty got lots of information, but just looking at her computer made her feel guilty. She hadn't written anything for her blog since Timothy's appearance on the radio. That was three days ago. She knew she should write, but she just couldn't. That made her about as bad as the people who didn't stop and think. She wasn't giving anybody anything to think about.

Gherkins! She did think about stuff! Patty sat down at the table and opened her laptop. After everything booted up, she navigated her way to *Wikipedia* in no time. There it was: *Gherkin from the Dutch word* gurkin *meaning pickle*. Pickle! Everybody already knew gherkins were pickles. Maybe gherkins weren't really worth thinking about.

Patty stood and put two slices of bread in the toaster. What did it really matter if she could outsmart a household appliance? The chance to get her blog more attention was already shot. She wasn't smart enough to do anything about that. No wonder she didn't feel like writing anymore.

Meanwhile . . .

"I got an idea," Fred Frost said.
Ed kept his head down at his desk in the cluttered

newsroom shared by everyone who worked on air at ASAP. He had no idea why they called it the newsroom. Nobody ever truly covered any news. He had just finished writing copy for a promo. *Tune in this evening at eight o'clock for Wayne Bender's* Sports of Every Sort. *Tonight, Wayne covers the International Blueberry Eating Contest from Middlebush, New Jersey. This year, in addition to the traditional muffin and pie eating categories, a new competition has been added: blueberry smoothies. Watch out for those ice cream headaches.*

"Did you hear me? I said I got an idea."

"Yeah," Ed answered. Maybe he didn't know why their workspace was called a newsroom, but he already knew from experience that nothing good ever came of Fred saying he had an idea.

"Here's the thing. We're gonna start streaming the show live on the worldwide interweb, right?"

Ed cringed as he nodded. Fred couldn't quite master the vocabulary of the digital age.

"We gotta have guests, right?"

"I'm working on it, Fred. With our budget, I've got to find people who are going to be in town, anyway. The pro rodeo is in the Garden in two weeks when we start the video streaming. I haven't got any cowboys, but I'm working on a couple of clowns."

"I'm way ahead of you in the clown department."

Ed's voice rose, "You've been talking to the guys I asked!"

"Calm down, Junior. I got my own idea. That Old Guard fruitcake. There's a clown for you, but the dimwits who listen to us loved the guy. Let's get him for the first show we webdo."

"What's a webdo?"

"You know what I mean wiseass."

"Yeah," was all Ed said. It wouldn't make any difference to point out that "loved" was a relative thing given that only eight-seven people voted in the Barnaby's Fishing Rods poll about the Old Guard. He did have to agree with the assessment that anybody who listened to Fred Frost on the radio was a dimwit.

"Well?" Fred asked.

"I don't know."

"What's to know? The guy is bound to say a bunch of stupid shit and get a bunch of laughs."

"But what about the money?" Ed asked. "He lives in St. Paul. If we want to spend money on travel, we should save it in case we get a chance at somebody good. You know, somebody connected to an actual important sports story."

"And do what in the meantime? Stream a blank screen?"

"We'll be there."

"Exactly. And who the hell are you? You've had this job for three months."

"I can count." Actually, Ed wasn't too sure about his counting. Three months already felt like three years—sort of like a prison sentence.

"Leave the numbers to me, Junior. Nobody else is gonna give that jerk time on the radio streaming all over the webnet."

"Right, the webnet."

"You're catchin' on. Don't worry, I'll get him for nothin' but a cheap plane ticket. We can put him in that dump across the street for one night. They said they'd give us a rate."

"Maybe."

"Forget the damn maybe. Go have Tiffany check about the room rate. See if she'll drag her ass over there to ask in person. Seein' that rack might get us a better rate."

"Is that what you want me to tell her?" Ed asked.

"Shit no! Are you crazy? Just go ask her about checking the price."

"Okay."

And Then . . .

As the newsroom door closed behind Ed, Fred picked up the phone and pushed zero. He got through on the fifth ring. "Hey, Tiff, I need you to call that Old Guard."

"Hey, Fre, I got a name."

"Jesus, Tiffany, don't be such a hard-ass."

"Mary Magdalene, Fred, don't be such a dumb-ass."

"Not her," Fred said.

"What?"

"I don't want that Mary. You know, his assistant or whatever the hell she is. She doesn't know a damn thing about sports."

"Patty."

"What?"

"Her name was Patty."

"Who gives a shit?"

"Hold on Fred. Ed is standing here."

"I know where Ed is. He can wait."

"How do you know where Ed is?"

"Maybe I'm psychic."

"Or an idiot savant," Tiffany said.

"Just get that Old Guard fruit on the phone."

Meanwhile . . .

Patty cut her tuna fish sandwich on toast in half. She opened the refrigerator and looked for something to drink. The carton of orange juice seemed all wrong for tuna. She had a little milk, but she needed to save that for her morning cereal. It was two days until grocery shopping night. She didn't just go running to a convenience store for milk. Doing all her grocery shopping on grocery night kept her budget right. That was a good rhyme, too.

Iced tea! She had instant iced tea mix in the cabinet left over from last summer. She pulled over one of the heavy dinette chairs and took the jar down from the top shelf. The dried tea dissolved into a glass of tap water. She had just filled the ice cube tray with fresh water yesterday. Iced tea would be perfect with tuna fish. She just knew it!

She took the ice cubes from the freezer compartment and twisted the tray. Nothing popped loose. She turned the tray over and bopped it on the counter. Three cubes skittered out. One cube liked skittering a lot. It landed on the floor. Great! She finally had the toast under control, and now the ice had to go crazy. Just as she put the two cubes from the counter into her glass, the Vikings fight song played on her phone. Patty retrieved the phone from the dinette table. "Hello."

"This is All Sports Athletic Programming, neighbors to The World's Most Famous Arena. I'm calling for the Old Guard."

"Yeah, uh, er, he's not here."

"Is this his associate?"

"Associate? Oh, yeah, right, this is Patty."

"I'm putting you through to Fred Frost."

Patty looked down and nudged aside the melting ice cube with her foot.

"Hey, Old, this is Fred Frost."

"Hello."

"Who is this?" Fred asked. "Is this that Mary?"

"Patty," Patty said.

"Well, look, I gotta talk to that Old Guard."

"He's not here."

"Well, why the hell not?"

"I assume he's working," Patty said.

"You assume? You don't know?"

"No."

"No, you know? Or no, you don't know?"

Patty didn't know what Fred Frost was saying

anymore or why they were having the conversation.

"You still there?"

"Yes," Patty answered.

"So what are you saying, anyway? Can you get me through to the Old Guard?"

"It'll take a little while."

"Are you his agent or something?" Fred asked.

"No."

"So he doesn't have an agent, right?"

"No."

"No, right? Or, no he doesn't have one?"

"The latter."

"Huh?"

"He doesn't have one," Patty said.

"Good. We don't pay any appearance fees. Just expense money."

"For what?" Patty asked.

"For being on the show."

Patty looked at her phone. The words had to be coming out of it even if they didn't make any sense.

"Are you still there?" Fred asked for the second time in the conversation.

"There weren't any expenses when you interviewed him," Patty said. "I have an unlimited calling plan, or, uh, I mean he does."

"Who cares?"

"I thought you did."

"I'm not talking about phone bills. Expenses to come to New York," Fred said. "We want him on the show. We need him in two weeks. That's when we start internetting live video."

"You mean on the web?"

"No, this is the whole enchilada, worldwide. Don't you know anything about the internetting?"

"I have a blog, er, uh, I mean Timothy does."

"Who the hell is Timothy?"

"The Old Guard. It's his blog."

"Well, tell Timothy this is not just some blog. We're streaming to the whole world. You know, everyplace, like France and shit."

"I don't know if Timothy speaks French."

"What the hell difference does it make? France is full of a bunch of fruits. Most of them speak English, anyway."

"Timothy makes a lot of French pastries."

"Why the hell are we talking about France?"

"I don't know," Patty said.

"Well, try to follow the conversation. We need the guy in New York to do the show."

Patty almost dropped the phone. "Uh, er, I'd have to come with him."

"Not possible. We don't have the money."

"He doesn't travel by himself."

"What does that mean?" Fred asked. "Are you trying to hold me up for a trip to the Big Apple?"

"Allergies," Patty blurted.

"What?"

"He has allergies."

"You mean he sneezes and shit?"

"No, food. It can be severe. I have to travel with him."

"What kind of food?" Fred asked.

"Well, um," Patty said. "Gherkins."

"Gherkins! Those are pickles."

"Right, from the Dutch word *gurkin* meaning pickle."

"Who the hell cares?"

"I have to . . . taste his food."

"Don't worry, this city's got plenty of pickle tasters. He might even like that about New York." Fred guffawed.

Patty had never heard anything like the obnoxious noise coming through her phone. It sounded like a guffaw.

"Look, I'll say it one more time. We don't have extra expense money. Tell him not to eat any pickles while he's here."

"It's not just pickles. It's the spices, uh, mace. He's allergic to mace. I can taste it in food." Patty didn't even know if they used mace in pickling.

"Hey, if he's that bad tell him to pack a lunch. We only got so much money. I think maybe you're allergic to hearing or maybe you got your own rash, like an itch to come to New York. So, scratch it on your own dime. You know, unless it itches in some real interesting place."

Patty wondered if there was a way to use mace on somebody over the phone.

"Look, lady, we need him on the show in two weeks. We're streaming live. I'm working on the set right now. Can you get him here?"

"Well—"

"I need an answer. If it's a go, I got four hundred dollars for expenses. Tiffany can call you about the arrangements. Can you get him here?"

"Sure. Of course, I have to—" Patty heard the line click on the other end. She was pretty sure the click happened as soon as she said sure. Of course, she wasn't really sure of anything.

CHAPTER SIX

The bus sighed as it came to a stop. Patty got up from her seat. She glanced down at the crushed corner of the flat white box from Creative Cookies. Even though she had the box on her lap when the huge guy got on the bus at the mall, he managed to spill over onto her seat as he sat down. His jam-packed bag from Jalapeño World tried to make friends with her Creative Cookies box. A big dent was the result. Patty pondered why the country had to be so fat as she stepped down to the sidewalk carrying the box with the giant cookie inside.

She stood in the sunlight and touched the box's corner. It didn't seem as much like a present in its present condition. She pushed out part of the damage, but a wrinkled crease in the cardboard remained. Her apartment was two doors down to the left. A bow! The drugstore was two doors up to the right. They would have a bow. That would make the box look better. She just knew it!

Patty hustled into the drugstore and found the gift wrap display. She saw a whole bag of regular bows for $3.25.

Of course, she didn't need a whole bag of bows. She didn't even like giving presents, at least not near as much as her dad did. She saw a row of single bows for $3.50 a piece! All they were was a little bigger and a lot frillier. Of course, the present was for Timothy. She grabbed a frilly green bow and headed for the counter.

"Creative Cookies," the clerk at the cash register sighed. "Oh, I just love them. They're so, uh, so, uh . . . creative!"

Patty was glad the woman was on the other side of the counter. She looked big enough to do as much damage to the box as the guy on the bus did.

"Is the bow for the cookie?" the clerk asked. "We have nice wrapping paper if the cookie is a present."

"Thanks. The bow is enough," Patty said. She hated wrapping presents. Anyway, she couldn't use up all her artistic energy on a package. She needed it for making logos. She just got a new job for the Friends of Solitude Association.

Patty paid for her purchase and walked quickly to her apartment building. She sat on a concrete bench at the entry and took the bow out of its package. She stuffed the cardboard backing in her jeans pocket to recycle. She studied the clear plastic dome for a recycling symbol. Nothing! She pondered why all plastic couldn't be recyclable as she put it in the trash can next to the bench.

She looked down at her box and pondered where to put the bow. She wasn't sure and took a moment to ponder why she was doing so much pondering today. It was too bad the huge bow still couldn't hide the damage done to the crushed corner. Maybe the opposite corner with the Creative Cookies logo was the best spot. She didn't think it was a very good logo, anyway. Purple wasn't a good color to go with cookies. Anybody should know that. Besides, Creative Cookies was kind of a competitor for The Sweet Shoppe. It wouldn't hurt to hide the logo. She had to get on Timothy's good side.

Meanwhile . . .

Timothy creased the last fold in the solid red wrapping paper he had chosen for the gift he was decorating. Wrapping the flat white box had been a piece of cake. He chuckled. Actually, it had a cookie inside. He took thin gold ribbon and strung it around the package lengthwise, then crosswise. He cut smaller bits of ribbon and tied them to the intersection of the larger pieces circling the present. With the flat edge of the scissors, he zipped the smaller bits into curlicues to make a bow just like his great-grandmother always did.

Mean, Meanwhile . . .

Patty let herself in the entry door and made her way up the stairs. She hesitated in front of Timothy's door and pondered whether to ring the bell or knock. She had to do everything right if this was going to work. She just knew it. A ring was more formal, but a knock might be more friendly.

Just as she lifted her hand to knock, Timothy's door swung open.

"Patty!"

"Timothy!"

"You surprised me," he said.

"*You* surprised me," she answered.

"Why?" Timothy said. "I live here."

"I mean opening the door."

"Oh, yes, of course."

They both stood there with flat, square packages in their hands.

"Dear me, where are my manners. Would you like to come in?"

"Yes."

"Well, yes, of course. Why else would you be at my door? Unless, of course, you were delivering something. Not to imply that you were bringing something to me. I wasn't trying to presume."

"I am." Patty would have pondered why she didn't say anything more, but she was tired of pondering things.

"Dear me, where are my manners. Would you like to come in?"

Patty was pretty sure Timothy had just said that.

"Patty?"

"Yeah. I mean, sure. I mean, thank you." She lifted up her box to give it to him, but his hands were occupied with the package he was holding.

"Please come in and sit down. Why don't you take a spot on the love seat. You can set your box on the coffee table."

She saw a small sofa upholstered in dark green cloth with some kind of woodsy pattern. Patty didn't know much about furniture, but it looked expensive to her. Little pixies or elves or something danced in between the trees.

"I don't know about you, but I just love love seats," Timothy said as Patty sat.

"Right."

"I suppose you could call it a settee," Timothy babbled. "I know my great-grandmother would have, but I like love seat. I guess I'm just being modern."

"Yeah, I guess so."

"Oh, just listen to me. I bet you think I'm babbling. Here you come to my door, and I hardly let you get a word in edgewise."

"Uh," Patty patted the box in front of her, "I brought a present."

"Why, you don't say." Timothy patted his own elegantly wrapped package as he settled into a wing chair with the same upholstery as the love seat. "Isn't that a coincidence? I was just coming over to your apartment. This is for you."

"Really?"

"Oh, dear me, yes. It's just a trifle to say I'm sorry for ruining your interview. I mean, of course, my interview trying to be you. Oh, heavens to Betsy, did I say that right? I'm afraid I just keep fumbling the ball, to put it in your parlance."

"It's okay." Patty lifted up her box. "I brought you this to say thank you."

"Oh, imagine that. Now you're just embarrassing me. I just can't take it until you open my package first. It's kind of an apology."

"No. I mean, I did almost kill you with cold medicine. I think you should open my thank you first. It's part apology, too."

"And now, you're just being a silly goose as my great-grandmother used to say. I insist. You open first."

"No, it's right for you to be first." Patty tried to think of another word for first in case the exchange continued.

"Dear me, a standoff." Timothy stood.

"What are you doing?"

"We'll just have to break the deadlock. We can flip for it." He opened a drawer in the end table next to the love seat and pulled out a small blue album of some kind.

Patty cocked her head.

"This is the most fun predicament. Sort of like the Gift of the Magi." He held the cardboard album against his temple. "Or maybe not, but I do just love O. Henry. Don't you?"

Patty did love the candy bar.

"Would you listen to me go on. What I mean is, this is a special circumstance. We should have a special coin. We can use one from my Buffalo nickel collection. Whattaya say?"

"Sure. Fine."

"You're the guest. You should call."

"Okay." She watched the nickel flip in the air and called, "Heads."

Timothy slowly uncovered the coin. The buffalo on the back side faced up. "Tails! I win."

Patty knew how a coin flip worked.

"Isn't this my lucky day! You come calling at my door. We get to exchange presents, and I win the coin flip. Here you go." He handed her the package and sat down again.

Patty took the box from Timothy and tore off the carefully wrapped paper. She saw a white box with a purple logo for Creative Cookies.

"It's a cookie," Timothy said.

"Right." Patty lifted the lid to reveal a big red-frosted cookie in the shape of a sports foam finger. In the middle, white icing spelled out *You're #1*. "Thank you."

"Well, I mean it. I've been boning up on my sports, and I keep seeing these big fingers in pictures. Of course, not as cookies. If I understand correctly, they're made out of foam rubber, though I imagine that is a misnomer. Surely, the foam is some sort of plastic, I should think."

"Right, plastic. Anyway, open yours."

"Oh, I intend to. This is such fun, but I have to tell you that I've also been reading *The Old Guard*."

"I haven't written anything in three days."

"Oh, I've just had a lovely time exploring your old columns. I am so impressed and I feel I'm learning, too. I had no idea college football coaches make so much money. And your piece on the length of basketball players' shorts! I thought it was a little spicy but very droll."

Patty was sure this was the second time Timothy had called her droll. She had a good memory for that kind of stuff. Like a photographic memory, except she didn't see it, she heard it. A phonographic memory! The term just popped into her head. Maybe she was droll.

"I see that look on your face," Timothy said. "You're wondering why I went to Creative Cookies. I'm sure I told you I don't decorate cookies at The Sweet Shoppe. That's Martin's bailiwick, and really, he's just wonderful. Unfortunately, there was a fly in the ointment, as my great-grandmother used to say. I thought our little adventure with my masquerading as the Old Guard was quite an amusing escapade. Well, of course, when I get started on a story, I can carry on. There I was telling Martin, and I happened to include the part about fainting on the floor from the cold medicine."

"Not good?"

"That would be the case." Timothy studied his hands for a moment. "Martin can be quite protective of me and perhaps a little dramatic. Not that I would call him a drama queen, but I just didn't think that asking him to make a cookie for you was the most prudent idea."

"Is he really mad?" Patty asked.

"Oh, I wouldn't worry about it. Martin has a good heart, and you have a good spirit. We shouldn't put too much stock in a little momentary tiff." Timothy scratched his head. "Hmm, for some reason, it doesn't seem like I should say tiff."

Patty pushed her package across the coffee table. "Here, open yours."

Timothy reached out to take it. "Oh, my, my, what's under that beautiful bow? That says Creative Cookies. I think we have to call this kismet."

Patty might have been droll, but Timothy seemed like a walking dictionary.

He opened the lid to see a big round cookie with a building pictured in frosting. "Well, what do we have here? Interesting."

"It's Madison Square Garden," she blurted. "You know, The World's Most Famous Arena."

"Oh." His face reddened.

Patty shrugged. "It's like they say on the radio. On ASAP."

"Oh my stars." Timothy stood and looked away. "Not that."

"It's okay. They liked you."

He looked back at Patty. "Really?"

"Really," Patty said. "That's why I got the cookie. To thank you."

"Who would have thought? I believe I do see the resemblance to Madison Square Garden, now." He leaned over to tilt the box toward Patty.

"They did it off a picture on the Internet."

"You don't say. Aren't the advances in cookie technology remarkable?"

Suddenly, Patty's head jerked back. "Wait, you actually know what Madison Square Garden looks like?"

"I saw it on a website in my research. I truly have been learning more about sports. I've just been so impressed with your passion about the subject. Maybe I saw the same picture on the Internet that Creative Cookies used. It's a little hard to tell."

Patty stared at the image on the cookie. It was probably about as good a picture as you could draw with frosting.

"Of course, I truly love the cookie. How thoughtful of you."

"Wait, there's more," Patty said. She sort of wished Timothy would sit down again.

"Another present?"

"Kind of," Patty's eyes glanced up. "A free trip."

"I beg your pardon?"

"All Sports Athletic Programming wants you to go to New York."

"Me? Whatever for?"

"They want you on the radio. I mean, not exactly you. You know, the Old Guard."

"Oh, dear."

"They want you in studio because they're starting to stream their show on the Internet."

"Oh, dear."

"They'll pay. I mean not money."

"You mean goods? I've read on your blog about athletes getting free shoes and such. I don't believe I need any athletic accoutrements."

"No, that's not what I mean. They'll pay travel money, just not a fee to appear."

"Travel money?"

"All your expenses."

"Oh heavens, you don't mean I'd have to go alone. I can't be the Old Guard without you." Timothy collapsed into the wing chair.

Patty jumped up in case he had fainted again. "Are you okay?" At least she hadn't given him any foreign substances this time. Thankfully, he hadn't even eaten any of his cookie. Who knew what kind of dyes they put in the frosting.

"I would say I am most assuredly not okay. For a moment, I was seriously considering continuing a hoax on the radio."

"It's not really a hoax," Patty said.

"What else could it be called."

"An, uh, uh, uh . . . an interpretation. You would just be interpreting my ideas. It would be an interpretation of the Old Guard. It would really help me."

"Well, I do like to be a good neighbor."

"Great! You're the best!"

"Oh, gracious me, no. No, I'm not."

"You're not going?" Patty collapsed onto the love seat. Timothy's furniture was taking quite a beating.

"I truly don't see how I could. I hate to mislead people."

"But think for a minute. I've got really good ideas. Instead of misleading people, couldn't sharing good ideas be leading them in a good direction?"

"I do try to be helpful to people."

"Of course you do! And you get to go to New York."

"Seeing new places is one of my favorite things. I've been to almost every new place in Minnesota."

"Huh?"

"Oh, yes. New Ulm, New Prague, New London, New Hope. There's quite a few in Minnesota. I haven't made it to Newfolden, yet. Isn't that a curious name? It's in the far northwestern section of the state."

"Right. Right. So New York's good. It's another new place."

"Well, not in Minnesota. Though we do have a New York Mills."

Patty didn't know how to get Timothy off his "new" kick. She half-wished she had some cold medicine with her.

"Listen to me prattle on, but you never did answer my question."

"What question?" Patty asked.

"You're right. I didn't pose it in the form of a question. I meant about going alone to impersonate the Old Guard. I couldn't possible do it by myself. Would I have to go alone?"

"No, no. That's the great part, I'll go along as your associate. It's a really good opportunity for me."

"Well . . ."

"You do like to be a good neighbor, don't you?" Patty asked. This was going to work out. She just knew it!

CHAPTER SEVEN

Patty put down her phone and opened her laptop. She needed to search for airline tickets on the bigger screen. Some woman at ASAP named Tiffany had given her a good tip.

Timothy had agreed to go to New York. ASAP still wouldn't pay for her expenses, but Tiffany said Fred Frost had budgeted $400 to pay for Timothy's travel. She told Patty to split up the money any way Patty wanted. Tiffany also said to check out Absolute AirLink. The airline's website came up as Patty reached into her wallet for her credit card. The banner at the top of the page read: Absolute AirLink – Pay Only for What You Absolutely Want. Patty absolutely wanted the cheapest tickets.

She clicked to the reservations page and her heart sank. Absolute AirLink had only one daily flight each way between Minneapolis and New York. They could already be sold out! She typed in the dates for the trip. They were leaving in exactly two weeks. She hit the arrow next to the box for the dates and a pricing policy page appeared.

Absolute AirLink is committed to helping its guests optimize their travel dollars. Fly with us and pay only to reserve your seat. The charges below apply only to services you Absolutely Want!

Checked Baggage: $25.00 per bag, click for size restrictions

Carry-on Luggage: $5.00 (one bag per guest), click for size restrictions

In Flight Beverage Service: Coffee, $2.00 per 10-ounce cup

Soft Drinks and Water, $2.00 per 20-ounce bottle

Beer, $4.00 per 16-ounce can

No food service is available. Lunch bags can be carried on for the low cost of $1.00 per bag, click for size restrictions

Ladies handbags free! (Gentlemen, too) click for size restrictions

All seats on Absolute AirLink are priced by location. Pay only for the location you Absolutely Want!
continue→

Patty scrolled to the arrow on her screen and tapped to continue. She scanned the diagram of the airplane seats to New York and back. She was in luck! The two worst seats on the plane were available on both flights. They could fly right across from the restroom each way! Only $151.38 per passenger. Tiffany had told Patty that she could get a room for ASAP's corporate rate at the Safe City Inn. A room for only $79.00. Tiffany had already told the hotel to expect a call from someone representing the Old Guard. Patty didn't even have to tell her Timothy's name. That was good. The less ASAP knew about either of them the better.

Name! Patty didn't know Timothy's last name. She couldn't make plane reservations without his last name. She had to get it. Those two worst seats wouldn't last forever. They could sell at any time! She rushed out her door and across the hall. She pounded on his door loud enough for everyone in the entire building to hear. No answer! She pounded again. No answer!

Patty looked at her watch. Four o'clock. She knew The Sweet Shoppe closed at three. There had been plenty of time for Timothy to get home. She needed to nab those lousy seats, but without a last name there was no way the reservation system would let her. Letter!

She ran to the stairs and bounded down two at a time. The mailboxes where people got letters had last names on them. There was the box. Apartment 2B! And the name on the little white slip of paper was? Smudged! All she could make out were the last three letters – don. Gordon? Condon? Cordon? Who had cordon for a name? This was hopeless. She spun around from the mailboxes and bolted face first into Timothy's chest.

"Oh, my," Timothy said. "So sorry. I should have alerted you to my presence. You seemed so intent on the mailboxes that I didn't want to interrupt."

"I need your name."

"Timothy?"

"Last name."

"Oh. London."

"Great. Meet me at my apartment." She bounded up the stairs two at a time.

Patty had left her apartment door wide open. She collapsed into the chair in front of her computer and tapped the space bar. The Absolute AirLink screen came up again. Perfect! The two worst seats were still available. She started clicking and typing as fast as possible. As she clicked away, she heard Timothy enter her apartment.

"Yoo hoo," he called.

"I'm in the kitchen. Make yourself at home." She glanced toward the living room and saw him sink into her chaise lounge lawn chair.

"Thanks," he said.

"There's some sports magazines on that box next to you. Maybe you should read one of those."

"A very appropriate suggestion. I have to admit to a certain apprehension about my sports knowledge. I just wonder how I'll possibly be able to do an in-person interview."

"You'll do fine." Patty's fingers slipped on the keyboard as she said the words. She had to backspace out the letters *nmzx* from the reservation form.

"Well, as I've said, I do like to be a good neighbor."

Patty finished the reservations. She had only heard a few "ums" and "ohs" out of Timothy as she switched to open the website for the Safe City Inn. She saw a dingy brick building with the letters SCI above a dirty glass double door. It looked like a place that ought to have the letters CSI on it for an episode of one of those crime scene investigation shows that she never watched. Tiffany had said that it was a chain of New York City hotels. Patty clicked quickly through the website and found its only two other locations in the Bronx. They looked worse than the first one. Still, $79.00 per night. It said right in the name that it was safe.

"How are you doing?"

Patty jumped in her chair. How had somebody as big as Timothy walked into the kitchen without her hearing? Was she that focused on the safety of the Safe City Inn? She didn't like that. After all, she was spunky.

"Did I interrupt?"

"No, no, you're fine," she said. "Almost done."

"Well, isn't that something? Just look how efficient you are."

Patty wrote down the phone number for the Safe City Inn and got off their website. "There. Sit down if you want."

"Why, thank you. I believe I will take a load off as my great-grandmother was fond of saying. I found some very interesting reading in your magazines." Timothy completely filled the sturdy oak chair on the other side of the table.

"Which magazine?"

"Which magazine, what?"

"Which one was helpful?"

"Oh, this one." He held out a slick-covered publication. "My heavens, it has a truly fascinating article about ballpark food."

"What?"

"Food. From all different cities and all different sports seasons." He turned a page. "Here, this one is even from Minnesota. Vikings chili. It says serve hot and steamy on a cold football Sunday."

Patty was getting a little steamy, herself. Why couldn't he read about linebackers or baseball pitchers or hockey goalies like a normal guy?

"It's a very clever recipe. It uses cod, which is very Norwegian, of course. Then those white Great Northern beans. And onions. And here's the real genius—yellow tomatoes for a beautiful blonde color just like all those handsome, blonde Scandinavian Vikings who took to the seas."

"Right."

"Oh, I'm waxing poetic, aren't I? I didn't intend to go on about blondes. I mean look at you. You have very lovely chestnut hair. And that pixie cut is cute as a button."

Patty's haircut was good for sports. That's why she had it. She never liked being called cute as a button. Still, it was hard somehow to stay mad at Timothy.

"Well, here I am going on, but I do love to read about food. They had a barbecued ribs recipe for the baseball team in Kansas City. Of course, that just makes sense, doesn't it?" He turned the page again. "Here's one that I took special note of. It's New Year's Eve eggnog for a basketball team called the Knicks. They're from New York."

"So I've heard."

"Oh, well, yes, of course you knew that, but I figured I better memorize the recipe since the interview is going to be in New York and all."

Patty took the magazine from his hand. "I think we'll have a lot to study up on before you go to New York."

"You mean before we go. I'm just going to be the best Old Guard that I possibly can, but I wouldn't be anything without you holding my hand. I'm so worried that I'll let you down again."

"We have a whole two weeks to get ready." Patty didn't want Timothy to worry. She was worried enough for the both of them.

"Gracious sakes, there's one thing I need to learn right away."

"What?"

"Your name. Now you know my name, but I don't know yours."

"Paris. Patty Paris."

Timothy slapped his thigh. "Oh, you can't be serious. Martin's name is Washington."

"So?"

"Well, we always say our names are two of the world's great capitals. Washington and London. Now, we've got Paris, too. Maybe we'll meet someone named Tokyo, next."

Patty tried to smile. They were about as likely to meet somebody named Tokyo as Timothy was to be ready to be interviewed about sports in two weeks. She was in trouble. She just knew it.

CHAPTER EIGHT

Patty scooted into the window seat of row twenty-two on the Absolute AirLink flight from Minneapolis to New York. The plane was kind of small to fly halfway across the country with a load of passengers. She thought little planes were used for connecting flights. Either way, she knew Timothy couldn't fit comfortably into the scrunched space next to the window. He was busy stowing his paisley garment bag in the overhead compartment. She had one in the exact same pattern that she never used. It was hanging in her bedroom closet. Her dad gave it to her three years ago.

Absolute AirLink had scanned Timothy's ticket at the check-in podium to add the five-dollar charge for his garment bag to their bill. Patty only had the ladies' handbag she bought three days ago at a yard sale. A purse didn't cost anything to carry on. Free! Timothy had already swooned over the black leather bag. He said it reminded him of one his great-grandmother had back when he was a kid. Patty didn't know anything about handbags, but it looked old. That was for sure.

Neither of them had checked any bags. She was happy they didn't have that expense, but Timothy had fussed over what she would do without any luggage to "carry your things." Patty had plenty of reasons to worry about the trip, but her "things" didn't even make the list. They were only going to be in New York for one night. The handbag had plenty of room for her wallet, comb, toothbrush, toothpaste, deodorant, fresh underwear, and a clean blouse rolled up neatly on top. If something got on her pants, she would just rinse it off at the hotel. Of course, she didn't actually have a hotel room. Given what ASAP was paying them for the trip, there was no way she could afford two hotel rooms. Timothy didn't know anything about that. He let her handle all the details of the trip. She'd have to figure out something about the room situation when they got to New York.

Timothy plopped down in the seat next to her. "Isn't this cozy. It's quite the cute little plane. And look, just two seats on either side of the aisle, I'd say it has a charming air of privacy. I can even hear Martin saying the same thing."

Patty glanced across the aisle at the restroom door. She didn't exactly know how Martin would have found their seats charming or cozy. Of course, she had never met Martin.

"Oh, my," Timothy said. "Did you hear me? 'Air of privacy.' It seems I've become an accidental punster."

Thanks to her logo work, Patty got tired of puns, accidental or otherwise. "Right."

"Dear me, you seem a little tense. I'm sure you needn't worry about the flight. I'll bet the safety record of these little planes is every bit as good as the big ones."

"I'm fine."

At that moment, the plane's speaker system interrupted them, which made Patty even better. The two flight attendants started their routine about buckling up, observing lighted signs, and the unlikely event of a water landing. Apparently, you didn't have to pay extra for any of these things—even using your seat cushion as a flotation device.

In the rear, where Patty and Timothy were seated, the roar of the engines stifled any chance for chit-chat as the plane took off and reached cruising altitude. Eventually, the captain assured them that they had leveled off and could expect a smooth ride to New York.

"Don't you just love flying?" Timothy chimed in.

Patty shrugged. "It's okay, I guess."

"You guess? I just think it's so much fun. Martin and I have taken several trips together. Not just business, either."

"I don't have much reason to travel." Patty looked past Timothy as the flight attendants rolled a small cart out of the galley at the rear of the plane.

A smiling blonde with the word *Absolute* strategically embroidered in red on her white blouse stopped the cart at their row. "Would you like something to drink?"

"No," Patty said.

"Are you absolutely sure?" the flight attendant asked.

Patty nodded her head. She wondered how a person could talk and keep a smile stretched that wide at the same time. Her colleague with the cart couldn't be a ventriloquist saying the words. Absolute AirLink would have charged extra for that.

"And what about the gentleman?"

"Perhaps a soft drink," Timothy said.

"We have twenty-ounce Pepsi products or bottles of water for two dollars."

"I believe I'll have a Diet Pepsi." Timothy chuckled. "I have to watch my girlish figure, you know."

Patty didn't see the point of making a joke to the woman. She was already smiling as much as humanly

TOM MCKAY

possible.

"Diet Pepsi it is. Last call for the young lady."

"How about it, Patty?" Timothy asked. "A bottle of water, maybe? It's good to keep hydrated when you travel."

"No, thanks."

Timothy looked back up at the flight attendant. "My great-grandmother always taught me the importance of drinking plenty of water."

"Is Diet Pepsi what you absolutely want, or should I switch you to a bottle of water?"

"Well . . ." Timothy dropped his tray table. "No, no, I shouldn't be such a diva taking up your time. I believe I'll stick with the Pepsi. Let's make the trip festive. Right, Patty?"

"Yeah, right."

The stewardess placed a bottle in front of Timothy. "Would you like a cup of ice for an additional dollar?"

Patty started to shake her head. They were paying for soda already. Who absolutely needed ice in it?

Timothy touched the barely cool bottle. "What a lovely idea. I believe a cup of ice would be just the thing."

The flight attendant put the ice next to the Diet Pepsi. "May I have your ticket please?"

Timothy handed it to her.

She ran a handheld scanner over the bar code. "All of your incidentals on the flight are added to a statement that will be emailed directly to your home or office."

"How convenient," Timothy said.

"At Absolute AirLink, you pay only for the things you absolutely want," the stewardess answered as she started to push the cart farther down the aisle.

Patty put her head in her hands.

"Not feeling well?" Timothy asked. "I wonder if you shouldn't have that bottle of water, after all?"

"I'm fine," Patty said.

64

"Well, I'm sure you absolutely know." Timothy chuckled again as he unscrewed the cap on the Pepsi.

Patty absolutely didn't want to hear the word *absolutely* again.

He poured his Diet Pepsi over the ice. "Don't you just love the fizzy sound pop makes? What would the world be without fizzy and fuzzy things?"

Patty didn't have an answer for that one.

"I think their prices for drinks are really quite reasonable, don't you? I mean we are captive consumers on an airplane."

"I guess."

"Am I being too much of a Chatty Cathy?"

"No, you're fine." Patty paused. "You're really better than fine. I mean, you really didn't have to do any of this."

"Well, believe you me, I gave it quite a lot of soul searching. I truly don't like to deceive, but I've read so many of the columns on your blog and I'm just so impressed."

"Thanks."

"Well, I mean it, and I'm just going to be frank. It's not fair to have stereotypes about people, and I know. Those guys on the radio weren't right to automatically believe you were a man just because you know so much about sports. They should be interviewing you, not me, so I think it's good enough for them if we pull the wool over their eyes a little bit. In fact, I'm sure those are just the words my great-grandmother would use. She knew how to fend for herself back in the days when it was a man's world. I'd say it's only right to follow her example." Timothy took a big gulp of his Diet Pepsi and poured some more in the cup.

"That's nice of you to say. I brought along extra copies of the columns I think they might ask you about. If you need them."

"Not to worry, there. I have the original ones you gave

me tucked safely in a big pocket in my garment bag. I've read them all twice and plan to study them again at the hotel, tonight. My performance should be much better than last time."

Patty looked over and saw a passenger pushing numbers on a keypad attached to the restroom door.

"Now, don't look surprised," Timothy said. "I have to remark that I've enjoyed reading your articles quite a lot. I haven't even opened the *House Beautiful* magazine I got three days ago. How about that?"

"Yeah, I guess that is something. Anyway, I talked to that Ed guy at ASAP. I'm pretty sure he's going to bring up the column I did on paying college athletes."

"I thought that one was particularly insightful," Timothy said. "The things I didn't know. And, imagine, I live right in a city with a Big Ten university."

"You liked it?"

"If you ask me, you were just marvelous at setting up the case. At first, it seems like the men's football and basketball players in college ought to be paid given all the money that their sports bring in. Then, you really lower the boom when you point out that that money is needed to pay for the non-revenue sports and that those athletes work every bit as hard as the football and basketball players."

"That sounded convincing to you?" Patty asked as she watched the passenger come out of the restroom and slam the door.

"I should say so. It was also a very good point that all scholarship athletes can get a free education, but the football and basketball players get the advantage of extra notoriety and connections because of the popularity of their sports."

"Wow, you really did study my columns."

"Well, I do want to get things right this time," Timothy took another drink of pop. "I also think the way you explained the role of revenue sports in funding compliance with Title IX relative to women's sports was just splendid. Make no mistake about it, I care about issues of equality and discrimination."

"You're fired up."

"Goodness. I am, aren't I? I may need another Diet Pepsi."

"Really?" Patty saw another passenger slam the restroom door.

"Just kidding," Timothy said. "Do you suppose that door is sticking?"

"I don't know. Looks like some people are just crabs."

"Well, there's no need for us to be grouchy. Just look at us. Paris and London are flying to New York."

Patty smiled. "I guess so."

"Isn't that just the fun of having a name like London?" Timothy chewed on the last piece of ice in his cup. "Oh my, pardon me, crunching away like that."

"That's okay. Lots of guys do it."

"I suppose you're right. That was the downside to having a name like London. Having to live up to a macho moniker."

"Huh?"

"My parents named me Timothy Jack London. My dad loved his books."

"I've read *Call of the Wild*," Patty said as the restroom door slammed again.

"My dad's favorite. He's quite the outdoorsman. I know he's wished I would have followed in his footsteps."

"I think dads try to do their best." Patty thought of all the presents her Dad was always giving her.

"I believe I did acquit myself reasonably well as a Boy Scout. I earned a merit badge for the Buffalo nickel collection I showed you the other day. I was also by far the best in my troop at tying knots."

"Really?"

"Oh, yes. It was actually a snap after all the macramé my great-grandmother taught me."

"Right," Patty said.

"Well, listen to me going on about myself, and you have a more interesting name than mine. Paris."

"I guess so."

"Oh, heavens yes. Paris, The City of Light."

"It's not so great when your first name is Patty."

"What's wrong with Patty? I think it's a charming name. It fits someone lovely like you."

"It's not the name. It's the initials. You know, Patty Paris, P.P."

"Pardon?"

"The kids in school teased me all the time. Pee Pee."

"Well, children can be cruel, but I bet you held your own. I know what it's like to be teased."

"But maybe not all the time. Pee Pee this. Pee Pee that. Who has to go Pee Pee? Pee Pee. Pee Pee. Pee Pee."

"Oh my, I wish you hadn't said it like that."

"That's the way it was." Patty remembered how hard she worked to get good at sports just to shut the other kids up.

"Oh, I surely do believe you. It's just that . . . well, that's what I have to do now. You know, twenty ounces of Diet Pepsi."

Patty nodded toward the restroom across the aisle. "I guess we're sitting in the right place."

"I've noticed that it has a keypad on it. I think I'll need the flight attendant to explain." He pushed the call button.

The walking smile made her way to Timothy's seat. "May I help you, sir?"

"I was wondering about using the little boy's room."

"I can provide you with the code."

"Well, isn't that just wonderful. I suppose it's that extra little bit of security."

"If you can hand me your ticket, please. The restroom is a twenty-five dollar charge added to your incidentals statement."

"Twenty-five dollars?" Timothy said.

"Only if you absolutely want to use it."

Patty touched Timothy's arm and gave him a pleading look.

"I absolutely have to go," he whispered to her.

She closed her eyes and heard the scanner beep as it registered Timothy's ticket. This was going to be an expensive trip. She just knew it.

CHAPTER NINE

"I almost wish we were staying on Staten Island," Timothy said as he walked with Patty to the front doors of the Safe City Inn.

"This place doesn't look that bad." She didn't think it looked that good, either.

"Oh, no, I was thinking of the ferry. Don't you just love ferries? And imagine, a boat ride to include in our journey. See, we started on a city bus to the LightRail stop. After that very convenient conveyance, we rode an airplane across the country. We got here and you were so clever to figure out the subway from the airport. So, that was another train ride, and then we had the trek on foot from the subway stop to here. All we're missing is a boat ride. The Staten Island Ferry is quite famous."

Patty glanced up at her smiling New York alter ego. "No bicycle."

Timothy's face fell. "Oh dear, you're right."

"Sorry."

He reached for one of the double doors. It didn't

budge. He pulled on the other one and held it for Patty as it swung open. "After you."

"Thanks." She wasn't sure whether the other half of the door was broken or locked. It might not have been a good sign either way.

"You are most welcome."

"I'll get us checked in. ASAP gave me all the information."

"Well, I'll just let you. I don't mind at all being pampered." Timothy eased down into one of the chairs in the lobby.

Patty shook her head. The metal-frame chair upholstered in aqua-colored vinyl didn't look anywhere near comfortable enough to pamper anybody. She walked over to the registration desk.

"Looking for a room?" a young man about her age asked from behind a thick plexiglass barrier. "Seventy-five an hour, two hundred a night."

"What?"

"The rates."

"By the hour?"

"Look, honey, I got eyes. He's got luggage. You don't. Seventy-five an hour or two hundred a night."

"Hold on." Patty raised her hands and waved them back and forth. "We've got reservations. I mean he does. For the Old Guard."

"The what?"

"ASAP made the reservation," Patty said. "The radio network."

"Oh, them. I don't have anything for any old, uh, you said—"

"Guard."

"Yeah, well, I don't have anything for an Old Guard." The man picked up a pen and began to twiddle it between his fingers. "All I got here is somebody named Paris."

"That's me. I'm Paris. He's London."

"Yeah, and this is New York."

"I meant he's the one staying in the room."

"It says Paris here." He tapped the pen against the desk. "You're Paris, right?"

"Right, but he's staying in the room. I'm his, uh, associate."

"I don't care which one of you stays in the room but, only one. You ain't associating in it. ASAP has the corporate rate for one person set up. They pay for one, one uses the room."

Patty nodded her head. This guy said one about as many times as Absolute AirLink said absolutely.

"Okay. I need your credit card for any phone calls and security. No smoking, no pets. You pay cleaning fees for smoking and any costs of pet damage."

Patty wondered if the clerk thought she had a gerbil hidden in her purse. She slipped her card in the metal tray under the barrier and watched him go through the check-in procedures. She signed the registration form and credit card slip that he slid back to her. She exchanged the signed papers for an old-fashioned key hanging from a maroon, plastic fob. Room 422. Twenty-two was her lucky number!

Timothy stood as Patty headed back in his direction.

"Got the key," she said. "You're in 422."

"Is your room close?"

"I checked you in first. You should get some rest. I didn't want you to have to wait."

"How considerate, but you didn't need to. I was perfectly comfortable."

Patty could see the lumpy lobby chair right in front of her. She felt a shiver of panic. Timothy clearly wasn't any good at lying. What was going to happen tomorrow?

"It did look like check-in was a bit of a struggle."

"Big city," she said. "Sorry it took so long."

"Oh, well, it gave me some time to study the lobby.

That ceiling fan looks like something out of *Casablanca*."

"Huh?"

"The movie. Don't you just love Ingrid Bergman? Oh, and Bette Davis. Those were the days of movies. Lauren Bacall, Judy Garland."

"Right."

"Well, anyway. Some of the things in this lobby are just fascinating. Look at that mahogany phone booth. How old do you think that is?"

"Old!" Patty blurted.

"What?"

"You have to look old! Remember? Rockdale High School? It closed forty years ago. What if anybody at ASAP looked anything up?"

"Oh, my stars, that is a dilemma."

"We have to make you look old."

Meanwhile . . .

Brandon sat in the tiny room at the back of the ASAP studios used to record promos and commercials. He was about to assume his stage name to cut a spot for Wayne Bender's *Sports of Every Sort*. Every time he used the name Ed, it made him feel out of sorts.

"Hi. This is Ed from the *Fred and Ed Show* here on All Sports Athletic Programming. I'm looking forward to Wayne Bender's *Sports of Every Sort* tonight as he travels to Wrightstown, New Jersey for the International Paper Airplane Championships. Glide on into your favorite comfy chair and listen to the action just like I'll be doing. Wayne describes every exciting moment from folding to flying to fame. That's Wayne Bender's *Sports of Every Sort* tonight at 7:00 p.m. on ASAP, neighbor to The World's Most Famous Arena."

Brandon leaned back in his chair. He got the thing in one take, right down to the neighbor of The World's Most

Famous Arena. Just once he wanted to say ASAP—in a former home of The World's Most Infamous Occupation. Of course, that wasn't really true. The studio had never been used for any conservative talk radio shows.

Right now, the *World of Lawn Bowling* was broadcasting from the main studio. He probably should have been listening in if he ever wanted to learn the differences between Bocce Ball and Rolle Bolle. He knew one was Italian and the other was Belgian. At least the show gave the network an international flavor.

International flavor sounded good at the moment. He could almost taste the marinara sauce at Mama Lunardi's restaurant. It was only two blocks away. He planned on having dinner there later. It would be his treat for the night. He knew he'd need one. In the morning, he had to help Fred put up the new set in the main studio while the recording of *Sports of Every Sort* was replaying. He couldn't imagine what Fred had come up with, but they started streaming tomorrow.

Mean, Meanwhile . . .

"Isn't this just the most marvelous thing? This old escalator with wooden treads. Why, I had no idea any such thing existed in Macy's. Oh, I wish my great-grandmother could have seen this. We used to watch *Miracle on 34th Street* together every year between Thanksgiving and Christmas. And now, here we are in the original R.H. Macy store. Aren't you just thrilled?"

Patty was thrilled that they were in a real store. They needed something to put gray in Timothy's hair. He had to look old! When they asked the clerk at the hotel if there was a pharmacy or variety store in the neighborhood, he sent them around the corner to a Quickie Market. That place didn't seem to have anything but bottles of booze, junk food, and cigarettes. Well, those things and condoms. Timothy had turned bright red at the condoms, but that only made him look younger. The place sure didn't have any hair care products.

"Goodness me, look, I think this is our floor. See. Cosmetics."

They had ridden up three flights of the escalator. Timothy looked like he was having so much fun that he might have preferred to keep riding up some more.

"Great." Patty tugged Timothy's arm as she stepped clear of the moving treads. "Let's see what we can find."

"I bet they have a marvelous selection." He motioned toward a vast array of store cases. "In fact, everything in New York seems marvelous. Did you see that billboard for *Hamilton*?"

"It was pretty big."

"My stars, yes. You could read it all the way across the square. Wouldn't you just love to see the musical? Everything you read says it's fabulous."

"I guess I'm not much on musicals."

"Oh, Martin just loves them. Of course, I do, too, but I have to say you're opening my eyes to a whole new world with sports. I even saved a little surprise for you."

"Surprise?"

Timothy beamed. "Two nights ago, I watched a baseball game on TV."

"Really?"

"Almost three full innings. Though I wish the pitchers could get a little better at putting the ball where batters could hit it, don't you? It's a lot more exciting when they're running and catching. I think so, anyway."

"Pitching is part of the game." She cringed at the thought of Fred and Ed asking any baseball questions.

"Oh, I know," Timothy sighed. "That and spitting. I don't know why they have to show so many pictures of that."

"Yeah, right. Anyway, we have to find something for

your hair."

Patty led the way through a huge display of ladies' perfumes. The ocean of scents could have hidden a city dump. Finally, she spied a poster in the distance of a hunky guy naked from the waist up.

Timothy must have spotted the same picture, "Look, I believe that's the direction we need to go."

Patty hurried their pace until they reached the hunky-guy poster.

"Now, that's advertising," Timothy said. "See, a whole array of body sprays. I wonder if I should try something?"

"We have to worry about your hair."

"Well, yes, of course, it's just that I left my sachet at home."

"Your what?"

"I have a little sachet with potpourri that I hang in my garment bag when I travel. It keeps my shirts fresh." Timothy flapped his shirt front.

"Potpourri?"

"I use my great-grandmother's recipe. Dried rose petals, lilac, mock orange blossoms, a hint of sage, and a single clove for good luck. I'm afraid the luck didn't work this morning. I left in such a tizzy that I forgot my sachet." He picked up a can of ocean mist body spray. "Hmm."

"Forget the ocean. You're supposed to be from Kansas."

They walked by a few more counters of deodorants and body wash until they reached the hair care section.

Timothy picked up a box. "This says it leaves just a touch of gray."

"That's if you already have gray hair."

"Oh, I know. You see the commercials all the time. I've just always wondered how it does that."

Patty scanned through the products on display. It seemed a guy could make his hair red, black, brown, blonde, or a bunch of other colors she had never heard of. Didn't anybody want to make their hair gray?

"Tut, tut," Timothy said.

Patty looked over. "What?"

He was pointing at a little slip of white paper on the front of a shelf. "It says Go Gray."

Patty squinted at the tiny print. "How did you see that?"

"There's one for each of the products," he answered. "I like to think of myself as quite the accomplished shopper."

It didn't matter. That spot on the shelf was empty. The Go Gray was gone!

"Look at this," Timothy said. "It's for frosted tips."

Patty pointed at the picture on the box. "We don't want to make you look like some surfer dude."

"No, of course not. Though, I dare say he is good looking."

"Yeah, whatever. I think this is hopeless."

"It's a shame we didn't think of this back home," Timothy said. "I'm sure my hairdresser could have fixed me up."

"Hairdresser?"

"Oh, yes. My Andre is a genius."

Patty sighed at the thought of the whole scheme she had gotten them into. She didn't feel like a genius.

CHAPTER TEN

"Here we go," Timothy said as he stepped outside of the Safe City Inn with Patty. "Off for a taste of New York. The choices really are difficult, aren't they?"

The choice of restaurant wasn't difficult at all for Patty. They took a little detour after their failed hair care mission at Macy's. She thought Timothy should at least see Madison Square Garden from the outside. Patty knew he would hear it called The World's Most Famous Arena more times than she could count the next day. Still, she didn't count on them walking by an expensive restaurant in a place that called itself an historic tavern. Timothy fell in love with it just by looking in the window.

Patty came close to falling, too—falling over at the prices on the menu posted by the door. She hadn't even gotten a room for herself, and she could see that they were going to spend more than the $400 in expense money that ASAP was paying. A pricey meal would only make it worse. Luckily, the clerk at the hotel had saved the day. He told them about a little mom-and-pop Italian restaurant around the corner that he said was really good—and really cheap. Maybe Safe City Inn wasn't such a bad name for the hotel. Her budget felt a little safer.

"Isn't this quite the adventure," Timothy said, "discovering a real neighborhood restaurant in Gotham?"

"Right." Patty didn't know what Gotham had to do with it. Maybe Timothy had seen some kind of advertising for a Batman movie. New York had posters, billboards, and marquees everywhere.

They walked to the corner and rounded it. They went past the Quickie Market and turned right again at the next corner. Mama Lunardi's was two doors down. Patty realized that it was really just the far side of the block from the Safe City Inn. Boy, New York had big blocks!

They descended two steps from street level and Timothy held the door. "How charming. A tiny little restaurant tucked away down here. Just look at the red-checked tablecloths and the candle stubs stuck in wine bottles. Even the wax running down the sides lends ambience."

"Uh huh, bottles." Bottles! That was it! Patty knew what to do.

"Good evening," said a dark-haired man with a white apron tied around his waist. "Two for dinner?"

"We don't have reservations," Timothy said. "Is that a problem?"

"Not at Mama Lunardi's. Mama doesn't take reservations."

Timothy turned to Patty. "See, isn't this just the most charming place?"

Patty held up two fingers to the waiter. "Two."

They followed the man to a small table in the corner. Of course, Mama Lunardi's looked like it was all small tables and corners. Patty didn't think the place could hold more than twenty-five people.

Timothy picked up one of the menus the waiter had

left on the table. "What a good idea to come here. The bill of fare looks so traditional. Spaghetti and meatballs, penne with shrimp and garlic butter sauce, Mama's lasagna. Isn't your mouth just watering?"

The waiter returned with a small loaf of bread and a glistening plate of olive oil with grated Parmesan. "May I get you something to drink?"

"Wine," Patty blurted.

"Goodness me," Timothy said. "Somebody's very decisive."

"You said we should make the trip festive," Patty answered.

The waiter tapped a pen against his order pad. "I see, festive. Perhaps the lady would like to decide on dinner before the gentleman selects a wine. Let me give you a moment."

Patty glared at the waiter as he walked away. Didn't he think a woman could choose a wine? Of course, Patty never drank wine. The corkscrew her dad gave her was still twist-tied to the piece of cardboard it came on.

"He probably treats the couples who come here like it's date night," Timothy said. "I'll bet he'd never guess we're here in New York on business."

Patty wondered if Timothy was a mind reader or just a nice guy. Either way, he was a nice guy.

"So, dinner, dinner, dinner. Would I be too unimaginative if I ordered the spaghetti and meatballs? I'm just so intrigued by the prospect of the marinara sauce in such a traditional eatery."

"That would be good. I was planning to order the spaghetti with marinara sauce." She had already compared prices. It was the cheapest thing on the menu. "That means a wine would go with both, right?"

"See, you do know your way around a wine list. Now, Lambrusco is companionable with Italian food, but I favor something a little more full-bodied. Possibly a

Chianti. "

Full-bodied sounded good to Patty. Maybe it would have more alcohol in it.

"Lost in thought?" Timothy asked.

Now, Patty hoped he wasn't a mind reader. "No, just thinking."

"Oh, well, hmm."

The waiter arrived in the middle of their non-conversation. "Have you decided?"

"Go ahead," Patty said to Timothy.

"I believe I'll have the spaghetti and meatballs."

Patty meant for him to order the wine. So okay, he wasn't a mind reader.

"And for the lady?"

"Spaghetti and marinara sauce, please."

"I see. Any meatballs, sausage, perhaps mushrooms?"

"No, just plain. And wine."

"We had discussed something red." Timothy fumbled with the wine list. "Here, a carafe of the house red should do nicely."

Patty wondered how much was in a carafe. She hoped it was a lot, but house wine sounded good. She was pretty sure that made it cheaper.

Timothy looked toward Patty. "Is the house wine okay? We could still consider an offering in a bottle."

"Perfect," Patty said. She knew the bottle she needed.

"Well, sometimes we do make the perfect team." Timothy turned his attention back to the waiter. "We'll have a carafe of this house red."

Patty looked across the room as the waiter left the table. For a second she thought some guy was watching her.

"Don't you think this is just the most romantic little restaurant? I'll have to tell Martin all about it."

"Right."

"I'll have to tell him about their efficiency, too. See?"

He nodded toward a door where the waiter was already returning with their wine.

The waiter poured a splash of wine in Timothy's glass. He sipped and nodded his head. The man filled Patty's glass next and topped off Timothy's, finishing each pour with a little flourish and making a graceful exit.

"Oops, I forgot something," Patty said.

"What?"

"My pill," she said. "It's in my room. I have to run back."

"Oh, dear."

"It's nothing serious. I'll just dash to the hotel."

"I should escort you."

"No, I can do it faster. You can relax. Drink your wine."

"Oh my, the wine. I hope it won't react with your medicine. You see the warnings all the time."

"It's not that kind of pill. I was rushing around this morning and forgot to take it. Like you and your sachet. Anyway, I have to take one every morning."

Timothy's face began to turn red. "Oh, I see."

"No, it's not that kind of pill, either. I'll run quick."

Meanwhile . . .

Brandon looked up from his linguine with clams. He saw a young woman rush out the door of Mama Lunardi's. He had noticed her before sitting across the room with some big guy. They were out-of-towners. It wasn't hard to tell. He was probably some oaf from Minnesota or Kansas who had just hurt his girlfriend's feelings.

Brandon went back to his pasta. That was the good thing about New York. Stuff was anonymous. Nobody in here was going to call him Ed, and he didn't have to worry about two people he was never going to see again.

Mean, Meanwhile . . .

Patty wobbled through the door of the Quickie Market. She felt a little dizzy. Maybe it was from the running. She thought she was in better shape than that. It couldn't have been the wine. She only had a couple of sips. Maybe the combination. She braced herself against the counter.

"Vlodka," she slurred. Maybe it was the wine.

The man behind the thick plexiglass barely looked up. "Along the wall."

Patty was impressed that the conversation took only four words. Maybe Timothy was right about people being efficient in New York. She was sure she needed vodka. Something clear-colored wouldn't show in Timothy's food. She scurried to the wall of liquor. The bottles were too big! She needed something to hide in her purse.

Patty hurried back to the register. "I need something smaller."

"What?"

"A smaller bottle of Vodka. Like a tiny one."

Without a word, the clerk reached over to a small rack beside a big display of cigarettes and produced a bottle that really was tiny. The guy definitely was efficient. He pushed it to her under the plexiglass. She slipped a twenty-dollar bill into the metal tray, and the clerk made change.

Patty tucked the bottle of vodka safely in her purse between the clean blouse and fresh underwear. She set off at a sprint toward Mama Lunardi's. She didn't want the efficient waiter to bring their meals before she got back to the table. She rounded the corner and popped down the stairs to the restaurant. As she entered, it sure seemed like the guy across the room was looking at her again.

Timothy stood as Patty reached the table. "Goodness gracious, you were quick."

"It was just a pill."

"Please, sit. Our salads are here." He pulled out her chair.

"I see you enjoyed a little wine." Patty took the carafe and topped him off, again.

"Thank you." As they sat across from each other, Timothy lifted his glass. "To sports."

Patty took a small sip. She used her fork to nudge two grape tomatoes to the side of her salad plate.

"Not a tomato fan?"

"Not anymore," she said.

"But you like marinara sauce. Isn't that just the way. Now take me, for example, I simply adore several Danish cheeses, but I can't abide cheese Danish. We only have it at The Sweet Shoppe to make Martin happy." Timothy popped a forkful of lettuce with a tomato into his mouth.

Patty dipped a piece of bread into some olive oil and took a bite. She hoped Timothy would concentrate more on the salad. A lot of bread might soak up some alcohol. "You want my tomatoes?"

"Are you sure?"

Patty nodded.

"Well, then, I don't mind if I do." He ate a tomato from her plate and followed with a swallow of wine.

Patty filled his glass once more. A guy with a hangover was bound to look worn out and older. This would work. She just knew it!

The whole efficiency deal also seemed to be working as the waiter arrived at the table with their plates of pasta. Timothy's had two giant meatballs in the center. He inhaled the aroma then sprinkled grated Parmesan over the top. Even better! That was bound to hide the taste of the vodka a little more.

Patty pointed over Timothy's shoulder. "Do you think that painting is by somebody famous?"

He turned to look. "Oh, the little print? Well, I'm just not sure."

Patty opened her purse, but snapped it shut when Timothy turned back quickly.

"I'm pretty curious," she said.

"Hm, let me ponder a little." He twisted in his chair a little for a second look. "I don't like to boast, but I made pretty good marks in art history . . ."

Patty reached into her purse and liberated the vodka bottle. She unscrewed the top and spiked his plate.

. . . of course, I don't think we gave the Italians their due. The professor spent most of the term on the French and Dutch. Now, it was just a night course, mind you, but I wanted my education to be a little more well-rounded than the curriculum at culinary school provided." He patted his stomach. "Not that cooking classes can't make you well-rounded."

"Right. That's okay about the painting."

"Are you sure? I do wish I could tell you more."

"That's okay. It's still a pretty picture." Patty lifted her glass. "To art."

Timothy took a drink then sampled his pasta. "This sauce has a lot of zip."

"Mm." Patty nodded.

"It's rather unique, but tasty. A good complement to the house wine."

"Have a little more," Patty said as she kept his glass full.

"Oh dear, I'm afraid I'm drinking more than my share."

"No problem. You could be right about my pill. Maybe I should go a little slow."

"Still, I don't want to be piggy."

"You should enjoy it. Plus, I bet your great-grandmother used to say 'Waste not, want not.'"

"She most certainly did." Timothy took another drink of wine. "Aren't we really getting to know each other."

"Right." Patty pointed over his other shoulder. "Is that

piece over the front door stained glass?"

Mean, Mean, Meanwhile . . .

Brandon stood to reach in his pocket and leave a tip on the table. The young woman was back with the big guy. She was pouring something over his dinner when he wasn't looking. The guy must have really pissed her off when she ran out. Maybe he'd hear something on the news tomorrow morning about a poisoning in Mama Lunardi's. That seemed a little overdramatic. She was probably pouring on some laxative or something. Anyway, those two weren't his problem.

CHAPTER ELEVEN

"Woo hoo," Timothy giggled.

Patty shook her head. Timothy was cheerful enough sober. If riding the Safe City Inn elevator gave him this much of a thrill, being drunk made him downright giddy.

"Thish ish bery uplifting." He snorted a laugh.

She had never heard him snort about anything. Maybe she overdid it at the restaurant. After getting him to drink most of the wine, it wasn't too hard to slip a little vodka into his coffee when he wasn't looking. He did notice the flavor. He thought maybe the restaurant put chicory in it.

He put his hand out as he swayed and touched the elevator buttons for floors five and seven. "Lo-ok, they all halve li-ul lightsh inshide." He snorted again.

Patty was just glad they were getting off at the fourth floor. The rum cake was probably a step too far. Timothy wanted the traditional cannoli. In his extra agreeable condition, it was pretty easy for her to change his mind to the rum-soaked desert.

The elevator stopped and the door slid open. Patty

gave him a little nudge. "Here we are."

"We-e are here." Timothy giggled. "Shlee shlame wordge."

"Right." Patty had to throw her arm out to keep the door from closing. "This is where we get off, big boy."

"I yam big, are-en't, I," he said as he weaved his way into the hall. He leaned back and stared. "Or, you're shmall."

"Shh." She put a finger to her lips. She didn't want to make a ruckus. So far nobody had paid any attention to them. When they came in, the night clerk at the front desk had been too busy playing some kind of noisy video game to even look up. Timothy quieted and leaned against her as they made their way to room 422.

"This is it," Patty said.

He reached for the door. "Ish shlocked."

"You have the key."

"Thas good."

"You want to give it to me?"

"Wha?"

"The key."

"Good hi-dea."

Patty waited.

Timothy stared.

Patty put her hand out.

Timothy shook it.

"The key," she said.

"Good hi-dea." He reached into his pocket.

Patty took the key and quickly opened the door while she had the chance. Inside was a double bed with a pink chenille spread on top. A small wooden desk and chair took up part of one wall. Beyond a narrow window, stood a matching wooden dresser. Timothy's paisley garment bag hung from a small rack on the wall. The red numerals of an alarm clock on the dresser glowed 7:45. Plenty of time to prep Timothy on some topics for his interview in the morning.

"Home again, home again, shiggity shig as my gr-eat grammuver would shlay."

"You want a glass of water or something?"

"No, jusht a li-ul resht." He collapsed on the bed.

"We have to talk about the radio."

"Jusht a sh-ort cat shnap." His eyelids were already fluttering.

Patty sat down on the desk chair. Her plan was working! Kind of. He was bound to have a hangover in the morning. A hangover would make anybody's face look haggard and old. Of course, she hadn't thought about this part of the hangover. The drunk part. There was no way he was going to study up on anything from her blog tonight. He had already started to snore. At least she wouldn't have to worry about not having a room for the night. Timothy obviously wouldn't notice if she just nodded off in her chair.

Meanwhile . . .

Fred's elbow bumped one of the two oversized plate stands holding the giant sheet of foamcore on his dining room table. He wished he could have worked on this thing in the kitchen, but that table wasn't big enough. That was the trouble with these old Manhattan apartments. None of the kitchens were big enough. Who the hell wanted to eat in the dining room all the time? He and his wife ate at a tiny drop-leaf table in the kitchen. They only used the dining room when they had company. Who the hell wanted company, anyway?

His paintbrush dripped a blurp of watercolor on the plastic tablecloth he had put down. He wiped it up quickly. His wife would chew his ass out good if he messed something up. He put a little more water in the brush and smeared it around in the brown color. The last time he used stuff like this was grade school. He was pretty good back then.

He took a half step back and admired his work. The building looked about right. He didn't know why they called it Madison Square Garden. The place was round! He'd outlined it all in black. The brown was highlighting the funny way the walls were built. How the hell did architects come up with shit like that?

A few more dabs of brown finished off the building. He rinsed out the brush and went back to work with the black to letter words onto the marquee. That was the best touch to the whole thing. He painted each letter carefully then stepped back again to get the full impact. A tiny tear of black paint dropped onto the dining room rug.

Fred tossed his brush in the paint kit and dashed into the kitchen for a wet sponge. His wife was off watching *Hamilton*, that musical everybody was always talking about. She wanted him to go with her. Who the hell wanted to go to a damn musical? He stayed home to paint the backdrop for streaming his show on the worldwide interweb. His wife was already ticked off that he stayed home. She'd do more than chew his ass if he didn't get that black spot out of the rug.

Mean, Meanwhile . . .

Patty stood up from the toilet and zipped her pants. It was a more comfortable place to sit than the hard wooden chair at the desk. She flushed and washed her hands. She didn't really think she could sit on a toilet seat all night.

She quietly closed the bathroom door behind herself and walked toward the dresser. She needed to set the alarm for five o'clock. They were due at the studio at six-thirty. Maybe she would have time to go over some things from her blog with Timothy in the morning.

The squeak of the bed frame broke into her thoughts.

She turned and saw Timothy lying on his side. He had rolled over to one edge of the mattress. Patty carefully lifted the free side of the bedspread and laid it over him. Maybe if she just used the edge of the empty side of the bed she could get some sleep, too. She pulled off her shoes and gently eased herself down. There was plenty of space between them. He'd never know she was there. She carefully evened out her breathing. She didn't think she snored in her sleep. This would work. She just knew it!

With a sudden groan, Timothy flipped over. As a big arm flailed toward her, Patty rolled away and tumbled over the side of the bed. She stayed on the floor, out of sight, and listened as Timothy's contented snoring started up again. Her position gave her a good look at the condition of the carpet. That settled one thing. Sleeping on the floor was out!

Patty stood and looked at Timothy's slightly disheveled, non-gray hair. She gently draped part of the bedspread over him again then sat in the desk chair. Patty crossed her arms on the wooden desk, laid her head down, and hoped for sleep to come.

CHAPTER TWELVE

Patty opened her right eye and looked at the alarm clock in Timothy's hotel room: 4:53. The crick in her neck chirped as she lifted her head. It was probably better than being crushed in the middle of the night by Timothy rolling around in his bed. She stood and reached over to shut off the alarm before it started chirping, too.

Light from the city sliced through the curtains drawn at the window. She took her purse into the bathroom and fumbled around for the toothbrush and toothpaste in the bottom. She brushed and thought about the day ahead. She needed to wake Timothy as soon as she finished getting ready. She took off her blouse and splashed some water on herself with her hands. She didn't want to use one of Timothy's washcloths. He thought she had her own room. The towels were another problem. She patted herself dry as best she could with a wad of toilet paper. Why couldn't the Safe City Inn even have a box of tissues? The blouse rolled up in her purse wasn't too wrinkled. She shrugged it on, changed into her fresh underwear, and combed her hair.

Timothy groaned into his pillow as she came back into the room. He was still sound asleep as she turned on the overhead light. He must have been having a bad dream. Probably one about a headache. Patty bent down and inspected his face. No new wrinkles, but it was kind of droopy. He probably looked a little bit older. Ashen, anyway. Ashes! That was it!

Patty clutched her purse and dashed out into the hallway. She rushed to the elevator and punched the down button. Why was the darn thing so slow? She ran to the stairwell and bounded down as fast as she could go, then scurried through the lobby and outside. A right turn and another right at the corner took her quickly to the Quickie Market. She was through the door and at the counter in a flash.

"Cigarettes," she gasped.

"What kind?" the man behind the plexiglass asked.

"Straight ones."

"They're all straight, lady. The only crooks we got are cigars."

"Nothing on the end."

"You mean no filters."

"Right."

"What brand?" he asked.

"I don't care. Whatever's cheapest. Two packages."

The clerk slid two packs into the tray. Patty put down her money and didn't even wait for her three cents change.

She dashed back to the hotel and straight to the elevator. She was panting too hard from the run to even think about taking the stairs. She pushed the up button and looked at her watch. She had time! She had time!

Maybe she shouldn't have had that thought. The elevator took *its* own sweet time to get to the lobby. When the elevator finally arrived, there was no Timothy to say "woo hoo" as it slowly started back up. It reached the fourth floor, and nothing slowed her down as she hurried to the room and unlocked the door. He was still sound asleep. She leaned down and shook his shoulder. "Timothy."

"Uhhh."

"Timothy, it's time to wake up."

"Uhhh."

"Please."

He rolled over on his back. His face looked drawn. The hangover worked!

"What time is it?" he groused.

"Five-twenty. You have to get ready."

"In the morning?" he moaned.

"Of course in the morning. You're going to be on the radio."

"Don't remind me." He closed his eyes again.

"That's right, you rest a minute. I have to do something in the bathroom."

"TMI," he mumbled.

"It's just cigarettes. I'll tell you in a sec."

Patty rushed into the bathroom and pushed on the little window at one end of the narrow space. She heard Timothy roll out of the creaky bed and follow her.

"This is a no smoking room you know," Timothy grumbled. "You could get us in trouble."

"That's okay. I'll open a window. Nobody will know. I'll fan the smoke out with a towel."

"Ugh. Smoke."

"Don't worry." She pushed on the window again. "Crap! It's stuck."

"There's no need for foul language." He gave the window a shove. He and the window both groaned as the sash slid up.

"Great," she said. Timothy must have been pretty strong. Maybe it was from kneading dough or something. Need! She needed something to put the ashes in. Patty looked back at the sink. Just two paper cups in flimsy plastic wrappers. She wanted to make some ashes, not burn the place down. She poked her head into the main room. Nothing!

Timothy followed her and leaned on the door frame.

"I gotta go," Patty blurted.

Timothy slid to the side. "TMI."

"No, just a quick errand."

"I don't feel so good," Timothy said.

"That's all right. You can rest." She was out the door before he could answer.

Patty looked at her watch. She moved as fast as she could. Stairs. Lobby. Doors. Right turn. Right turn. Quickie Market.

The clerk looked up as Patty braced herself against the counter.

"Ash tray," she fired.

"Behind you."

Patty turned but didn't see anything.

"Top shelf."

She looked up and saw a tiny ceramic toilet stool with the words "Put Your Butts Here" painted in red.

"Is that the cheapest one you've got?"

"It's the only one we got," he said.

Patty lifted up on her tiptoes and took down the ashtray. The clerk rang up her purchase, and she put nine dollars in the tray. She didn't even wait for the six cents in change.

Patty ran back to the hotel. She reached for the door then did a quick about-face. It was less than a minute back to the Quickie Market. The clerk met her eyes as she barged through the door. He pointed down, and Patty saw the plastic lighter in the metal tray.

"It's the cheapest one we got," he said.

Patty tossed down three dollars and didn't even wait for her dime change. The jog back to the hotel took more than a minute, and she panted in the elevator as it slowly delivered her to the fourth floor. She was breathing about as hard as somebody who did smoke cigarettes.

Timothy was hunched over sitting on the edge of the bed when she returned. "You're back," he said.

"Yeah, I've got to make some ashes, quick." She held up her purchases.

"I better do it," he said.

"But the smell."

"It might be an improvement."

"Huh?" She paused. "Oh."

Timothy took the lighter and the tiny toilet ash tray into the bathroom.

Meanwhile . . .

The crushed corner on the foamcore didn't look too bad to Fred. The interweb picture probably wouldn't even show it. The camera would be focused on his painting of Madison Square Garden, not some dented corner. The damage wasn't his fault, anyway. His wife Ubered him an SUV with some tall broad driving. Fred didn't see the rake off to the side when he shoved his painting into the back of the big Suburban. Who the hell Ubers around New York City with garden tools? He backed through the door of the ASAP office with the painting jammed under one arm and an oversized plate stand in each hand.

Tiffany looked up from her desk. "What the hell is that?"

"It's the set. The backdrop. Madison Square Garden."

"You could have fooled me."

"We're always saying that bullshit about neighbor to The World's Most Famous Arena, so here it is." He leaned his picture against the wall and put down the plate stands. "We start streaming today on the world wide interweb, if you even give a shit."

"Don't remind me." Tiffany pointed at the big sheet of foamcore. "You realize the corner's messed up, right?"

"I had a problem with a broad with a rake."

"What was she, an art critic?"

"No, it was in her car. She was doing Uber."

"You mean she was driving?"

"Yeah, a tall skinny broad."

"Skinny and broad at the same time. That's a pretty good trick, Fred."

"I didn't say anything about doing tricks. She had a damn rake in her car."

"I'd say she had two rakes."

"I just told you it was one."

"Look in the dictionary, Fred."

"Huh?"

Brandon walked in from the studio.

"Hey, Eddie boy," Fred said.

"You know, Ed will do just fine since it's not my real name, anyway."

"Okay, it's Ed, Ed," Fred said. "What's your damn problem? Out late last night? Hung over or something?"

"If you'll notice," Tiffany said, "he beat you here."

"Yeah, well, I had to transport the set."

"What is it?" Ed asked.

"It's Madison Square Garden. What the hell do you think it is?"

Ed thought it looked like an air filter for his Subaru. Actually, a dirty one like oil change places always showed you when they replaced it.

"I even put the marquee on it," Fred said. "See, Knicks Play Tonight."

"Kinks," Ed said.

"What?"

"Kinks," Ed repeated. "It says Kinks."

Fred stared at his painting. "Well, who the hell cares? People are supposed to be looking at us. Nobody's going to notice. It's just the backdrop. Anyway, it's all the same letters."

"Except for the 'c'," Ed said.

"What?"

"Knicks has a 'c' in it."

"So what is this, the National Spelling Bee? Wrong network, Eddie boy. Better get on air at ESPN—as if that's happening."

"What about the dent?" Ed asked.

"What about it? A rake did it."

Tiffany looked up from her computer. "I was just trying to teach Fred about rakes."

Fred turned his back to Tiffany and mouthed the word bitch.

"Leave me out of it," Ed said. "How are you going to put it up?"

"It fits on these stands. We just put them on a table behind our chairs and boom—a set."

"If we had a table," Tiffany said.

Fred turned to face her again. "What do you mean if?"

"Seriously, Fred, when have you ever seen a table that big around here? You think this is some church basement reception hall or something?"

"Well, maybe we can hang it from the ceiling. You got any string or bobby pins or shit like that?"

"Bobby pins." Tiffany laughed. "Good luck with that. You'll have to rummage around in your great-grandmother's purse or something."

"Then what the hell are we going to do?"

"We?" Tiffany said.

"Look, this streaming interweb is big for everybody. Ed, you're part of this, too. You think some damn thing up. I made the whole set."

"Uh . . ."

"Ed, open the storage closet next to the bathroom." Tiffany pointed to the door. "There's two big cardboard boxes in there. Get 'em both."

Ed followed her directions before Fred could call him Eddie boy again. "Hey, these are light."

"It's two cases of toilet paper," Tiffany said.

"Why the hell do we have two cases of toilet paper?" Fred said.

"With two cases, you get a free box of tissues," she answered.

"That's nothing to sneeze at," Ed said.

"Like I give a damn. You can't hang this up with toilet paper."

Tiffany twirled her hands in the air. "Turn the boxes on end."

Ed followed her instructions.

Tiffany stood up and put a plate stand on each box. "Just get everything in position and that will be your World's Most Famous Arena."

"Hey," Fred said. "I think this will work."

Mean, Meanwhile . . .

"I hope this will work," Patty said.

Timothy had made a mini-toilet bowl full of ashes, taken a shower, and dried his hair. He gave a deep sigh. "Me, too. I'm still a little rocky."

"You gonna be sick again?"

"Maybe a little something in my stomach would help. Not too much."

Patty remembered somebody saying tomato juice was good for a hangover. "I could run to the Quickie Market."

"My great-grandmother always gave me soda crackers to settle my stomach, or sometimes a little bit of cinnamon toast." He sat down on the wooden desk chair.

Something sweet! Patty had heard that was good for a hangover, too. "It would only take me a minute."

"Well, if you don't mind."

102

Patty was out of the room, down the stairs, through the lobby, and done with her two right turns as fast as she could make it.

The clerk at the Quickie Market didn't look surprised at all when she dashed through the door.

"Got any juice?" she squeezed out between breaths.

"Juice?"

"Tomato juice."

"You're serious?" the clerk asked.

Patty took that as a no. "Something sweet?"

"You're standing next to the candy bars."

"No." She didn't think they'd have any that tasted like homemade cinnamon toast. "More like a sugar cookie or sweet roll."

"End of the aisle."

Patty moved toward the back of the store where she saw a small rack with pork rinds, cheese puffs, and barbecue potato chips. There were some packages of cheese crackers. She didn't think jalapeño cheddar would work. At the very bottom, was a cellophane package of something called Yummy Buns. The gooey white frosting looked sweet. She took the Yummy Buns to the counter and paid for her purchase. She waited for her quarter in change. After all, a quarter was a quarter. Timothy hadn't moved from the wooden chair by the time she got back to the room.

"I found something sweet," Patty said. "It's not your great-grandmother's cinnamon toast, but maybe it will help."

"Oh, thank you."

Patty slid the package of Yummy Buns, which she had never heard of before, in front of the only professional baker she had ever met.

"Yummy Buns," he said.

She nodded.

Timothy tore open the cellophane and took a bite. He

chewed and swallowed. "Well, yes. What they can do with preservatives these days certainly allows things to stay on store shelves."

"Would you like a glass of water?" Patty asked.

"That would be a good idea."

She walked into the bathroom and took the plastic off of one of the paper cups. She saw Timothy's wet towel lying on the floor. His great-grandmother probably wouldn't have let him get away with that. He probably wouldn't have done it either if she hadn't loaded him up with alcohol last night. She filled the cup with water and carried it out to him.

"Thank you. I'll just wash down a few more bites."

Timothy finished half of the Yummy Bun and all of the water then walked into the bathroom to rinse his hands. Patty stared at the ashes for a minute until Timothy came back.

"I certainly hope you won't tell Martin about this," he said. "If he got wind of me with some Yummy Buns in New York City, I'd never hear the end of it."

Patty had never even met Martin. "Don't worry, your secret's safe with me. Here, sit down again. I have to do your hair."

Timothy sat while Patty dipped her fingers in the tiny toilet bowl. She worked a few ashes into his hair.

"Ooh," he said.

His hair started to look a little gray. She tried a few more. She thought he actually had nice hair. It was thick and sort of wavy, not like her plain old straight hair. She blended more of the gray ashes into the brown. It needed just the right amount. She dusted a few extra sprinkles on top as she thought about Andre the hair genius. Maybe she wasn't so bad herself. This was going to work. She just knew it!

CHAPTER THIRTEEN

Patty had pulled her agent act again to check Timothy out of the hotel. They were crossing the street headed toward a side alley like Tiffany, the woman at ASAP, had told Patty to do.

"I hope I'm up to this," Timothy said.

Patty hoped so, too.

"I just haven't been myself on this trip. Forgetting my sachet. Letting you take care of everything while I just gawked at New York. I know what my great-grandmother would have said. 'Take it easy, breezy.' I can almost hear her."

"It's okay."

"No, it's not. And last night. I don't know if you noticed, but I was pretty tipsy. I had my heart set on studying more of your columns." He sighed. "I just feel like a failure."

"You'll do fine." Patty reached over and squeezed his hand.

"Oh, part of it is that Fred guy. I don't like his tone—

the way he has to call me Old. I mean, your blog is called *The Old Guard.* Would it hurt him to call me by name?"

"They don't know your name." Patty stopped at a gray metal door with the letters ASAP painted in black. "Let's try to keep it that way."

"See, there I go mis-communicating already. I meant he should use the full name from your blog."

"Maybe I can mention it to Ed." Patty did want the proper name used. She pushed the button on an intercom mounted to the wall.

A scratchy "yes" sounded through the dirty plastic intercom cover.

"It's the Old Guard here for the *Fred and Ed Show,*" Patty answered.

The intercom gave a weak buzz and a latch clicked. Timothy held the door then followed Patty up a narrow set of wooden stairs. They emerged into a small reception area with a stunning brunette sitting behind a gray metal desk.

"Good morning. I'm Tiffany," the woman said.

"Hi, I'm Patty Paris. We talked on the phone. And this is Tim-iffany, er, uh, Tiffany this is the Old Guard."

"Pleased to meet you," Tiffany said. "Would you like to hang your bag on the hall tree?"

Timothy put his paisley garment bag on a hook. "Isn't hall tree such a wonderful term? My great-grandmother had a beautiful antique hall tree right by her front door. I just think the name is just so evocative. The idea of a tree growing right up in the house to be at your service."

"Sometimes I just say coat rack," Tiffany answered.

"Ah, well, yes, I guess you don't really have a hall here."

"Did you two sleep all right?"

From the expression on Tiffany's face when she asked, Patty figured she and Timothy looked like hell.

"I was out cold," Timothy answered.

"Like a log," Patty said. She could just as well have said on a log.

Tiffany waved aside their comments. "I know that place doesn't exactly provide luxury accommodations."

"But, very conveniently located," Timothy said.

Tiffany shrugged. "I'll get Fred and Ed in here."

Timothy clasped his hands and looked away.

She opened the line into the studio. "The Old Guard is here for the show."

Meanwhile . . .

Dave Kuberski, the station engineer for ASAP, pushed the button on his console to answer Tiffany. Making her wait for anything was never a good idea, but he had a couple more things to finish if the cockamamie live streaming was actually going to happen. "Give us a minute more. I'll have them right out."

"I wonder what the hell the fruitcake looks like," Fred said.

"There's no picture on the blog," Ed said.

"I thought everything was on the webnet."

Dave held up both hands. "Forget that you two. Just remember to keep the chairs in tight. Fred's so-called set is only eight-feet wide."

Brandon looked at the three office chairs in front of Fred's version of Madison Square Garden. The "set" gave them a little less than three feet of space each. He tried to divide that amount of space into the $65,000 he borrowed in student loans for journalism school. He wasn't good at math, but it had to be more than a thousand dollars an inch.

"Now look," Dave said. "These chairs are on wheels. Don't go moving around, or you might just roll off the screen. Put the guest in the middle, and Ed, you clip on his mic."

Brandon stared again at the three armless chairs crammed in front of a piece of foamcore. He wondered how big the Old Guard was. Maybe they would have been better off scheduling a jockey instead of a former football player.

"Okay, Ed," Dave said, "you've still got the dump button if anything has to be bleeped out. It's set a little lower now to be out of the camera frame. Works exactly the same, it's just a different position. If you have to bleep something, hit the button just like always."

"What do I do?" Fred asked.

"Try not to say something Ed has to bleep."

"Funny."

"Who's kidding?"

Ed held up a sheaf of papers. "I've got my reads. The commercials and the promo for *Sports of Every Sort*. How do I do these with the camera on?"

"I've got stills to put up when you have a read. Just say something like 'now a word from Barnaby's Fishing Rods' or 'coming up on Wayne Bender's *Sports of Every Sort*.' I'll put up the right still, and you read from your papers. The camera on you won't be live when the stills are up."

"So, the interweb's off?" Fred asked.

"No, the stills go out on the web during the reads."

"I never heard of stills," Fred said.

"Just let Ed do it." Dave pointed to the door. "Go get your guest."

Fred grumbled while Ed walked to the door first. He pushed it open and standing in front of Tiffany's desk were the big guy from Mama Lunardi's restaurant and the woman who had been trying to poison him. If it really was poison, it must have been the slow-acting kind. If it was a laxative like Ed guessed, he definitely hoped it had been the fast-acting kind. Either way, the big guy looked like hell. Actually, the woman didn't look so good herself.

"What the hell are you standing in the door for?" Fred asked from behind.

"Oh, it's nothing."

"Okay, then let's do something. Let's meet this fruit."

Timothy and Patty both looked over at Fred and Ed.

As the duo came closer, Tiffany stood up. "Fred and Ed, this is Patty Paris and, um—"

"The Old Guard," Patty said.

Ed reached out and shook Timothy's hand. "Nice to meet you. It's funny, I didn't find your actual name during my show prep."

"Tim-uthy, um, er, Burr . . . yes, Timothy Burr."

"Well, we're glad to have you here. And, of course, you too, Ms. Paris."

Patty just stared at Timothy. At least he came up with a fake last name.

"I'm Fred Frost, executive producer of the *Fred and Ed Show*." He shook Timothy's hand. "Huh, firm grip."

"Oh, well, you know. Old football player and all."

"Great," Ed said. "Here's the thing, we have to get you into the studio and miked up. We've got about six minutes. Right now, we're re-airing last night's *Sports of Every Sort*."

"Oh, yes, the show with your Mr. Bender." Timothy nodded his head vigorously. A flake of ash fell on his shoulder.

"Is that him up there?" Patty pointed toward a large, framed photograph on the opposite wall. She flicked the ash off Timothy's sport coat when the others turned their heads.

Fred turned back. "It says so in great big print."

"Right, right," Patty said. She didn't care for the Courier typeface. She never used it in any of her LoGo ToGo jobs.

"He's covering the International Fitted Sheet Folding Championships from Bedminster, New Jersey, but the show's about to wrap up," Ed said. "We've got to get in the studio."

Timothy nodded his head again.

Patty scanned for any loose ash as he followed Fred and Ed through the door. Not a fleck out of place. Everything was going to be all right. She just knew it!

"Ms. Paris, would you like to sit?" Tiffany motioned to a chair next to her desk. "If I turn the monitor, you'll be able to watch the whole thing streaming on my computer."

"Thanks, I mean, I don't want to interfere with your work."

"Not a problem. Your Old Guard is the only guest we've got today. If you watch on my screen, it gives me ten minutes free. I could use the break."

Ten minutes! Patty had never thought about the time. That was all the time her ideas were getting for flying on Absolute AirLink, staying at the Safe City Inn, and running back and forth to the Quickie Market. Ten minutes!

Mean, Meanwhile . . .

Ed clipped a mic on Timothy's lapel and pointed toward the center chair. "We want you in the middle so that it's easy for both of us to talk to you."

"I see, of course, very clever."

"Once you sit down," Fred said, "don't go getting light in the pants."

"I'm not sure I catch your meaning. You know, my great-grandmother had so many wonderful old expressions, but I don't recall that being one of them."

"I think what Fred is trying to say is don't roll around in the chair. We have to stay in the camera frame."

"In front of the set," Fred said.

"Oh, yes, the set. My, my, I always find naïve art so

very intriguing."

"Naïve," Fred said. "I guarantee you I know a hell of a lot more about Madison Square Garden than you do."

"Gracious, yes. You must be very well informed in your line of work. I certainly wouldn't presume to compare my knowledge. Why, at first I didn't even recognize the building."

"Take a good look." Fred gestured with both hands. "I painted the whole damn thing myself. Even put the marquee on it."

"Dear me, I see. The Kinks. I imagine hundreds of famous groups have had concerts in Madison Square Garden."

"Whatever," Fred said.

"Of course, The Kinks were before my ti-yping class."

"Typing class?" Ed said.

"Right, typing. You know, back in the day so to speak, those good old high school times back in Rockdale. We all had typing class. We'd sit and type away. Clackety-clack, clackety-clack. I can't tell you how many times I listened to The Kinks on my Walkman."

"They had those back then?" Ed asked.

"Oh, Walkman, like the radio. Yes, good question. No, that was a later device, of course. I had one of those little radios."

"You mean a transistor," Fred said.

"Careful Fred, you're dating yourself," Ed said. "What did you mean, Tim?"

"Right, right, what indeed. My walk, man. You know how teenage boys are, always practicing their walks. Sometimes, I'd listen to The Kinks."

"Your walk, huh," Fred said. "Talk about light in the pants. I hope you don't show us that one."

"Never mind that," Ed said.

Fred scowled. "Never mind tellin' me to never mind."

Ed held up one hand and tapped his earpiece with the

other. "Fred, the countdown. Dave's about to give you the cue."

Fred twisted his scowl into a smile. He turned to the camera, waited a beat, and said, "Good morning sport fans and welcome to the *Fred and Ed Show* on the All Sports Athletic Programming network, neighbor to Madison Square Garden, The World's Most Famous Arena. I'm your host Fred Frost joined by Ed Brandon. This is a special day and we have a special guest. Tell us all about it, Eddie Boy."

"Thanks, Fred. You can always be counted on for your usual introduction. And, speaking of introductions, we are excited to introduce a whole new way to enjoy the *Fred and Ed Show* as today we begin streaming our program live, for the first time, on the World Wide Web. Just go to www.asap.nttwmfa.com. With us today, by popular demand through the Barnaby's Fishing Rods poll question, is Mr. Tim Burr, known to many of you via his sports blog, *The Old Guard*. Welcome, Tim."

"Thank you."

"Welcome's the good word here." Fred said. "I'd like to welcome everyone watching on the worldwide, uh, netweb. Good, so, anyway, we do have the Old Guard here, and I'll tell you, this guy's full of opinions. Right, Old?"

"I do try to share ideas. Not that I want to take too much credit. I can't tell you all the people who know more than I do."

"Tim, I think you're being too modest," Ed said. "Your blog is very knowledgeable about a variety of sports. Given the recent scandals about big money in college sports and back door deals for college coaches, I'm sure we'll want to delve into your recent column about paying college athletes."

"Just don't tell us too much about back door deals," Fred snickered.

"Maybe we *should* start with a couple of more general questions," Ed interjected. "I've noticed that you blog a lot about football and basketball, but not so much about baseball. With baseball season in full swing, will we be seeing more on that?"

"Well, right, baseball. Our national pastime, of course."

"Some people think that's changing," Ed said. "I wonder what your thoughts are?"

"Now that you mention it, I was watching baseball just the other night. It seems to me that better equipment might help the game. Have you noticed how many times batters adjust their batting gloves? Heavenly days, you'd think that professional sports teams could afford better handwear."

"Handwear, huh?" Fred said.

"Oh, it isn't just that. Think about the bats. They're trying to hit a round ball, and they have a rounded implement. Don't you think it would be more sporting if they had a better chance to hit the ball? Maybe a bat with a flatter surface would help."

"You mean like cricket?" Ed asked.

"Isn't that the game the Indians are so good at?" Timothy said.

Fred threw up his hands. "Old, in case you haven't noticed, the Indians play in the American League. MLB. Major League Baseball."

"Heavens to Betsy, isn't that humorous. I just read about India's national team winning the world cricket championship, and, of course, you were thinking about the Clevelanders."

"Yeah, you're a laugh a minute, Old."

Ed shifted his notes in his lap. "Anyway, Tim, we are interested in your views about paying college athletes. It seems from your blog that you're strongly opposed."

"Gracious, yes. I don't think enough people realize

that the so-called revenue sports are needed to support the expenses of other athletic endeavors at universities."

"But is that fair?" Ed asked. "Football and basketball players bring in most of the money through their sports. They work incredibly hard. Don't they deserve a cut? Their coaches are certainly handsomely rewarded."

"Oh dear, fairness is a very big part of the question. All the wonderful progress for women's sports under Title IX is made possible in large part by athletic departments sharing revenue between sports. I was just reading an article in *Women's Sports Journal* about that very subject."

"So the women get treated by the guys," Fred said. "Sounds like going on a date."

"I don't think that's a very apt analogy," Timothy said.

"Probably a situation you're not familiar with." Fred winked at the camera.

Ed tried to keep his chair from rolling as he shifted his weight. "Maybe we're getting off point here. But, how should the athletes in revenue sports feel?"

"Dear me, I think they might feel fortunate. In addition to the scholarships that they get, as do athletes in other sports, they get to travel more, appear on television, gain more notoriety, have larger training staffs. It's quite a long list of benefits that don't come with other sports. The *Women's Sports Journal* was quite clear on these matters."

"They pay the freight," Fred said. "They ought to at least get to ride in the front of the truck."

"Paying the freight, as you say, might be part of preconceived notions. I was watching television just last week. College softball is a wonderfully fast and exciting game played by women. I dare say that universities might well make that into a revenue sport with the kind of promotion they give to football."

"Hey, Old, I thought you were a football guy."

"Dear me, I don't mean to sound disloyal. Still, my great-grandmother always taught me the Golden Rule. I bet my britches that given the same resources, a women's sport could be put on equal footing with one of the men's."

"An interesting take," Ed said. "Though I'm not sure it's practical."

Fred waved an arm. "Practical, smactical. Women's sports aren't going to generate the big bucks like the men do."

"I have to say that *Women's Sports Journal* opened my eyes on that subject, too. In professional tennis, the women's side often creates more interest and income in this country than the men's game. That got me to thinking about a smaller example from our good neighbors in northern Wisconsin. There the World Lumberjack Championships draw just as many spectators for the women's bracket as the men's. There was a feature article in my local paper. I should add that both do the exact same events: crosscut sawing, axe chopping, and even log rolling. I'm given to understand that it's quite exciting."

"So what do they call them? Lumberjills?"

"My, my, Mr. Frost," Timothy said "You're very prescient this morning. I've also read about the additions of diminutives or genteel modifiers to nicknames for women's sports teams. Would you believe there are actually teams called the Spartanettes and the Lady Stags?"

"What's wrong with Lady Stags? And don't call me precious."

"Prescient, Fred," Ed said. "I'm sure Tim said prescient. I believe he intended it as a compliment."

Timothy nodded and a flake of ash landed on his cheek.

"For our listeners just joining us," Ed said, "we are speaking with Mr. Tim Burr who blogs about sports as the

Old Guard. Let's open up the Upstate Maple Syrup hotline for your questions and comments. That's Upstate Maple Syrup, The Slowest Syrup in the East and sponsor of the *Fred and Ed Show* on the All Sports Athletic Programming network, neighbor to The World's Most Famous Arena."

"So, Old, you used to play football, and now you're telling us about lumberjacks. You don't exactly strike me as the lumberjack type."

"Heavenly days, I didn't mean to present myself as an expert, but it might be an excellent outing for the *Sports of Every Sort* show that I've heard advertised."

"In Minnesota?" Fred asked.

"Wisconsin," Timothy said.

"You're a real card, Old, if you think you're going to get Wayne Bender out of New Jersey." Fred slapped Timothy on the back.

Flakes of ash drifted down to the tip of Timothy's nose. His head dipped forward then shot back with a violent sneeze. Madison Square Garden, The World's Most Famous Arena, began to tumble from the impact of Timothy's gray-haired head. Ed dropped the sheaf of papers in his lap as he grabbed in vain for the falling sheet of foamcore. It landed on the floor, producing a matching dent to its opposite corner.

"What the hell!" Fred said.

Ed fumbled for the dump button too late to bleep out the last three words streaming into cyberspace on the World Wide Web.

Mean, mean, meanwhile . . .

Patty watched in horror as the words *Upstate Maple Syrup: The Slowest Syrup in the East* and a caricature of a turtle holding a bottle over a stack of pancakes filled the computer screen in front of her. She had heard and seen all of it. The studio mics were live before the show when Timothy babbled on about The Kinks and typing class and his Walkman. After the show started, she had crossed her fingers and hoped that Timothy would stop talking about cricket. She had nodded along when Timothy stood up for women's sports and clenched her fists each time Fred winked at the camera. And then . . . she cringed . . . and cringed . . . and cringed each time a bit of ash fell out of Timothy's hair. Now, she just stared at the stupid turtle pouring syrup on a stack of pancakes. She could forget about anybody ever taking *The Old Guard* seriously again. She just knew it.

CHAPTER FOURTEEN

Patty turned her head away from Timothy's snoring and looked out the window of the Absolute AirLink jet. She absolutely didn't care about the view. What she absolutely wanted was to wake Timothy up and have him apologize for snoring. Why not? Since the *Fred and Ed Show* calamity, he hadn't done anything but apologize. At ASAP, he apologized to Tiffany who was laughing too hard to hear. He apologized to Ed who was putting his papers in order before rushing back into the studio. Timothy apologized through the bathroom door to Fred who had locked himself in after grabbing the newspaper.

On the subway, Timothy apologized to a woman who banged his ribs with her huge backpack and an obnoxious guy who rammed into Patty exiting the door. He even apologized to a TSA agent at the airport for having a paisley garment bag. Throughout it all, Timothy kept apologizing to Patty mostly for just being himself. Maybe he didn't owe her another apology, but she still wished he would wake up so she could talk to him.

Meanwhile . . .

Emily Whittaker stared at the subject line going viral on the Internet. *Tim Burr fells Madison Square Garden #advocate for women's sports.* She hated her job as assistant to the associate producer for social media on the *M-M-M-Morning* show. She spent all day searching Internet posts and keeping track of hits on the social media sites for Molly, Myra, and Meg. The three co-hosts made everything a competition, and somehow, it was Emily's fault if one got ahead of the others in social media reactions. It would be worse if this women's sports thing mattered and Emily missed it.

She clicked a link on her screen and saw a big guy with gray hair talking to two other guys about lumberjacks. They were sitting in front of something that looked a little like the dirty air filter from her Subaru that the oil change guy showed her the last time she had her car serviced. On her screen, the talk was all about women lumberjacks and some contest in Wisconsin. Suddenly, the big guy reared back with a sneeze and knocked over the picture of the air filter. In a second, an ad with a turtle and a stack of pancakes appeared. She recognized the name Upstate Maple Syrup. They made it in a little town near the university where she went to journalism school.

Emily re-watched the video and searched some other sites to get a better idea of what they were discussing. She backtracked to check the number of hits on the video and read some posts about it. Sometimes, she got so sick of her job that she wanted to hit somebody with a post. At the moment, that didn't make much difference. She was pretty sure Molly, Myra, and Meg would be interested in this. She sighed and watched the number of hits on the video continue to explode. She paused for the brief thought that maybe she could rise in the *M-M-M-Morning* show hierarchy by moving the "E" in her name and becoming Miley.

Another look at the big guy knocking over the dirty air filter snapped her back to reality. The person sitting on the right was Brandon Edwards, that cute guy a year ahead of her in graduate school. It clicked. She remembered that he got a job at the All Sports Athletic Programming network. It wouldn't hurt to call Brandon Edwards and find out about this Tim Burr and what any of it had to do with Madison Square Garden. Actually, it wouldn't hurt to have any excuse at all to call Brandon Edwards.

Mean, Meanwhile . . .

Timothy flinched at the sound of the Absolute AirLink lavatory door slamming. His eyes fluttered open.

"You awake?" Patty asked.

"Well, uh, yes, uh, something did wake me."

"The bathroom," she said.

"Heavenly days, how did you know?"

"I'm sitting right here. How could I not know?"

"That I have to go to the bathroom?"

"Oh. Oh! I thought you meant the door. About every other person slams it."

"I don't mean to be indelicate, but I do need to use the facility."

"One or two?"

"Dear me, uh, um, one."

"Can't you hold it? We're supposed to arrive in twenty minutes."

"Well . . ."

The Absolute AirLink cabin speakers chimed for no charge. "Folks, this is the Captain. We've started our initial descent into Minneapolis. Everything is clear sailing in front of us. We should have you at the gate on or ahead of our scheduled arrival time. We hope that you've had an absolutely wonderful flight and that you'll join us again soon on Absolute AirLink."

"There, see. You can wait." Patty said.

"Well . . ."

The speakers chimed for free again and a flight attendant spoke, "As we make our descent, all passengers must remain seated with their seat belts securely fastened. We will be passing through the cabin to pick up any trash. All loose items must be placed in the trash bags carried by your flight attendants. Please have your tickets out to scan for the trash removal fee. Remember, all trash is disposed of for the absolutely low charge of only fifty cents per item."

"You *can* wait, right?" Patty asked.

"Well, of course, yes. I wouldn't dream of being a rule breaker."

"Yeah, you've already broken enough stuff today."

"Oh, what a ghastly thought," Timothy moaned. "I'm so chagrined by it all."

"Sorry," Patty said. "That was a joke."

"I fail to see any humor in my performance."

"I've been waiting to talk to you about that." Patty laid her hand on his wrist. "Your performance, what you said today. It was really good."

"It was?"

"All the things you said about women's sports. Those were really good points."

"I'm afraid I have to credit *Women's Sports Journal* for that, but I have been trying to bone up."

"You must have worked really hard."

"Some of it was quite interesting. As my great-grandmother used to say, 'Knowledge is its own reward.'"

"Not just the reading," Patty said. "You watched a lot of sports in a real short time. I mean, cricket?"

"Oh dear, I just tried to avail myself of the sports channels on cable. I had no idea there were so many. With so little time to prepare, I believe you could have called me a binge watcher."

"I don't see how you did it all, but you came up with some good ideas."

"What a marvelous thing of you to say. I wonder if that flatter bat for baseball wouldn't work."

Patty scrunched her face. "I was thinking more about when you said women's softball might be made into a revenue sport with the right promotion. That never really occurred to me. You really hit on what equal opportunity actually could be."

The airplane slowed to lose altitude.

"Gracious sakes, thank you. And then to think, I went and messed the whole thing up. My lands, I'm truly so sorry."

"It's not your fault," Patty said.

"Good heavens, I knocked over the whole set. And then, there was the swearing and the laughing and the, well, just the everything."

"I was the one who put ashes in your hair."

"But maybe if I hadn't overindulged so badly last night."

"That was my fault, too."

"I can hardly make my drinking your responsibility."

"I spiked your food."

"What!" Timothy's voice raised an octave as the airplane touched down hard on the runway.

"I didn't go back to the hotel for any pills. I bought vodka at the Quickie Market."

"Dear me." Timothy shook his head.

"I'm sorry. I poured it in your sauce and even put some in your coffee. I feel bad about it. Really. I thought a hangover would make you look older. You know, kind of worn out."

"Ah, I see. It seemed to me that my stab at chicory in the coffee was quite a reach. Well, this goes to prove what I've thought."

"You were on to me?" Patty asked.

"Oh, heavenly days, no. I had my head in the stars all of yesterday in New York, but it proves that you're every bit as clever as I thought. Imagine. Me with my trained palate, and you completely pulled the wool over my eyes."

Timothy started to laugh so hard that Patty thought he might snort again.

Mean, mean, meanwhile . . .

Brandon closed out of the journalism department website for his graduate school. He knew he remembered Emily Whittaker when she called from *M-M-M-Morning* in the afternoon. Sure enough, the picture fit as he read her profile in the online directory of alums. Her profile didn't say anything about a husband. Of course, that didn't rule out a boyfriend. He didn't care. He was going to call her back, anyway. Mama Lunardi's would be a good place for a first date. If she turned him down, it couldn't be any worse than the Old Guard versus Madison Square Garden disaster that had already happened.

So . . .

Patty listened to the voicemail on her phone as the plane came to a stop at their gate. Timothy had already complimented her on not pulling out her phone until the flight attendant announced that use of electronic devices was permitted. He unfolded from the airplane seat to retrieve his paisley garment bag from the overhead compartment.

"Wait!" She reached over and grabbed his arm. "They want us back in New York."

"Surely not on this plane. My stars, I can't imagine that Fred and Ed would ever want to see us again."

"No, not them. Just sit a minute. It's something called *M-M-M-Morning*."

Timothy plopped down. "The talk show?"

"I guess."

"That's a major network program," he said.

"I know. That's where the call came from."

"But you don't watch the show?"

"Not really," Patty said.

"But you have?"

"Not ever. It doesn't make any difference. The message said that Molly, Myra, and Meg are very interested in your views on women's sports."

Passengers filled the aisle, jostling carry-ons out of the overhead compartment. A large duffel bag slammed against Timothy's shoulder. Apparently, that was free of charge.

"Just one thing," Patty said, "who are Molly, Myra, and Meg?"

"Oh my, you truly don't watch. They're the co-hosts. They're really quite popular."

"You sure?"

"Positive."

"Good." Patty pumped her fist. This was better than ASAP. She just knew it!

"Ooh," Timothy said as Patty's fist pump hit his other shoulder.

"The message says we'll have first-class plane reservations for seven tonight if we confirm." Patty held up her hand before Timothy could speak. "Also, not on Absolute AirLink."

"Oh, thank heavens."

"Right," Patty said. "Get your bag. We've got a lot to do."

CHAPTER FIFTEEN

Patty sat in a fancy upholstered chair that matched the rest of the fancy lobby of the Waldorf Astoria hotel. She needed a better word than fancy. Timothy would have the exact right word, but he couldn't help at the moment. He was busy checking out at the registration desk.

The last twenty hours had passed like a whirlwind. As soon as they landed in Minneapolis, Timothy rushed to the men's room. With no time to spare, they hailed a cab. Timothy must have been one of Andre's good customers because he arranged an emergency appointment straight from the airport. Timothy's hair looked kind of nice with gray in it. He was right about Andre being a genius.

From the salon, another cab ride took them to their apartment building. Timothy chose fresh clothes and even remembered to put the sachet in his garment bag. For the first time ever, Patty took the garment bag her father had given her out of the closet and used it to carry her things. Now, the two paisley bags were draped together over the back of a sofa in the hotel lobby. Patty sort of liked that their bags matched.

The first-class flight from the Twin Cities actually fed them dinner. A limousine waiting at LaGuardia Airport delivered them to the Waldorf Astoria. The hotel's bar, with its classic dark wood paneling, was still open. Timothy said he would just die if they didn't go in, but all he ordered was a ginger ale. Patty figured that was probably a pretty good choice and joined him.

"Lost in thought?" Timothy asked as he sat down in a chair facing her.

"No, just thinking."

"Well, yes, right. Perhaps you're as nervous as I am. I do hope I acquit myself better today."

"You'll do fine." Patty silently tried to convince herself of that. "Just don't say too much about your walk. Or typing class. Where did you come up with that?"

"Oh, the typing. My great-grandmother taught at the high school before she was married. Typing, shorthand, all kinds of useful skills back in her day."

"And what about the name? Burr? I mean, where did you get that?"

"It just popped into my head. I saw that billboard for *Hamilton*, and everybody says it's just the most wonderful musical."

"Right."

"Of course, I didn't want anyone to see through my ruse." He sat up a little straighter in his chair. "I thought 'Don't say Hamilton.' So, I chose his nemesis instead."

"Burr."

"Precisely." Timothy beamed.

"Tim Burr?"

Timothy sighed and slumped back in his chair. "Um, well, yes, that was an especially unfortunate moniker when I knocked over Madison Square Garden."

Patty shrugged. "It got us invited back out here."

Timothy straightened up again. "See, that's what I

love about you. You're such an optimist. It puts me in mind of all the game shows I used to watch on television with my great-grandmother. All those contestants thinking what a wonderful chance they had to win the grand prize."

"I never watch those."

"Gracious me, I don't either anymore. I suppose some things in life just go away, but I do enjoy looking back. Oh, heavenly days!"

"What?"

"Looking back! That's what my great-grandmother did. She was always so annoyed that the game shows we watched came from California. She thought it was ever so much more glamorous when they came from New York. I can still hear her telling me that the guests on her favorite show always stayed at the beautiful Waldorf Astoria hotel. Wouldn't that be just the bees' knees if she could see us now?"

Patty nodded. "I know you miss her."

A moment of quiet lingered between them until the main door of the hotel opened. A young woman walked in their direction and stopped where they were sitting. "Mr. Burr?"

"Pardon? Oh, yes, right, of course." Timothy smiled as he stood.

"I'm Emily Whittaker from the *M-M-M Morning* show. There's a limo waiting outside. I'm the one who found you, so they sent me over today."

"Dear me, I didn't know I was lost."

"I found the video of you on the Internet. I'm the assistant to the associate producer for social media."

"My stars, what an impressive title."

"Right," Emily said. "Anyway, this must be your agent, Ms. Paris."

Patty had already stood from her chair.

"Good grief," Timothy said. "Where are my manners?

I should have introduced you."

"That's okay. We don't have much time." She handed them each a clipboard holding several sheets of paper. "This is our standard contract. Ms. Paris, they told me that you both have to fill out a contract if the payment is going through you as his agent. If we are paying Mr. Burr directly, then only he has to fill out a contract."

Patty handed back her clipboard. "Just pay straight to him."

The opening notes from *Wrecking Ball* sounded from Emily's backside.

Patty recognized the song. She liked Miley Cyrus.

Emily reached into a back pocket for her phone. "I've got to take this."

Timothy looked down at the form on the clipboard. "Oh dear."

"What?" Patty asked.

"They want my Social Security number."

"So, write it in."

"But, it also needs my name and address."

"How else are they going to pay you?"

"Heavenly days, Patty. They think my name is Tim Burr."

"Oh. Right."

"I just don't think I could defraud the federal government with spurious information. I shudder to think of the consequences. I can't imagine I would do well in prison."

Patty could see the beads of sweat forming on his forehead. "So put in your real name."

"But—"

"Just go ahead and do it. They won't even notice until later. It'll be somebody in some office. They won't care."

Timothy followed her advice and filled in the boxes. He completed the simple pieces of information just as Emily returned from the other side of the lobby.

"Sorry," Emily said. "I have dinner plans tonight. Just confirming the time. We're going to a little Italian place called Mama Lunardi's."

"Good heavens, what a small world. Patty and I were just there."

"I've been told the food's really good."

"I can't tell you how delightful mine was," Timothy said.

Emily took the clipboard from him and scanned the paper. She turned the form back toward him. "It says London on here."

"Yes, that's correct."

"Correct how?" Emily said. "I thought your name was Burr."

"No, London."

"So you're London and this is Paris."

"Right here in New York," Timothy said.

"But you're not named Burr." She stared at him with her hands on her hips. "Then, where did that name come from?"

"You might find that quite amusing."

Patty waggled her hand and shook her head to Timothy as Emily continued to stare in his direction.

"Um, well, it's because of winter," Timothy said. "Yes, the winter. Heavenly days, I just can't tell you how cold it gets back in Minnesota. I don't mind saying that I don't care for it. So, um, you see, it's just something my friend Martin started calling me in jest."

"Burr?" Emily said.

"That's right." Timothy gave a little shake of his shoulders. "Brr. Tim Brr. And, of course, you can see the irony, what with me living in Minnesota."

"So, it's a nickname," Emily said.

"Yes, yes, that's it exactly."

Patty could see another disaster shaping up. She just knew it.

Emily sighed. "Well, it's going to have to do for today. The promos and the script all have you as Tim Burr. Anyway, we have to go. The limo's outside. It's only a few blocks to the studio."

Meanwhile . . .

Tiffany looked up from her desk as Fred walked into the ASAP reception area.

"Hey, Tiff," he said.

"Wayne Bender's here," she answered.

"Here?"

"Yeah, here. He owns the place."

"You think I don't know?" He picked up the newspaper from her desk. "He's never here this early."

"Well, he is today." Tiffany took the newspaper back. "He wants to see you."

"Me?"

"What did I just say? If I were you, I don't think I'd keep him waiting."

"Yeah, yeah." Fred turned and walked down the hall toward Wayne's office. He stuck his head in the open door. "You wanted to see me, boss?"

"Yes, Fred, I do. Come in and close the door."

Fred pulled the door shut behind him and stepped toward the empty chair on the opposite side of Wayne's desk.

"You don't need to sit," Wayne said. "This won't take long."

"Okay."

"I watched the video of your show yesterday—"

"Listen, boss, it wasn't my idea to have that fruitcake on."

"We'll get into that in a minute." Wayne placed his hands on his desk and leaned forward in his chair. "I wanted you to know that I've taken one of your suggestions to heart."

"You have?" Fred said.

"You were quite pointed about expanding the geographical scope of *Sports of Every Sort*. You specifically mentioned the number of episodes that take place in New Jersey. I believe you have a good point."

"I do?"

"Yes, and as a result, I've taken steps to have *Sports of Every Sort* report on the Iditarod."

"Iditarod?"

"Yes, the dog sled race in Alaska."

"Right. I know what it is," Fred said.

"Good," Wayne responded. "You'll be covering it. Tiffany is working out the travel plans for you to be in Nome in January. She says there's a new outfit called Absolute AirLink that can get you to Seattle economically if you manage your expenses. You'll be on a limited budget. She's working on the remaining arrangements. I believe you can count on her to take care of you."

"But—"

"No buts, Fred. I'm taking you up on your idea. As to the rest of yesterday's show, I've always considered it an honor to be a neighbor to The World's Most Famous Arena."

"Yes, sir."

"While I find it remarkable that anyone could identify your so-called set as Madison Square Garden, unfortunately some people did. That kindergarten artwork crashing to the floor was an embarrassment to this network and disrespectful to the Garden."

"Yes, sir."

"Oh, and Fred, one more thing as you leave."

"Yes?"

"Your live streaming."

"Yes?"

"It's dead."

CHAPTER SIXTEEN

The seats for the audience at *M-M-M-Morning* were pretty comfortable. They put Patty in the front row while Timothy stayed in the green room. She didn't know why they called it that. It wasn't green at all. It looked like beige to her.

Some technicians were putting a wireless mic on Timothy, when a guy who worked on the show took Patty to her seat. She should have known Timothy would be ticklish. The last time she saw him, he was wiggling around while they slid a microphone wire under his shirt.

The first part of the show was just Molly, Myra, and Meg making dumb small talk and unfunny jokes that the audience laughed at anyway. They announced that the first guest would be the Internet sensation who had knocked down Madison Square Garden while standing up for women's sports. Now, the show was running a commercial for an air freshener as Timothy was being seated with Molly on one side and Myra and Meg on the other. He settled in and Patty saw a red light from one of the cameras come on.

"Welcome back," Myra said. "We are absolutely delighted to have our first guest with us today. He is Mr. Tim Burr, who has everybody talking about the way he managed to bring attention to women's sports."

Everybody in the audience but Patty laughed.

"Sounds like our audience is familiar with your work, Tim," Myra said. "Should we call you Tim?"

"Or Mr. Burr," Meg asked.

"Or Mr. Tim," Molly followed.

Everybody in the audience but Patty laughed.

"Oh, just Timothy, please."

"Ah, I see." Myra patted him on the hand. "Formal, but not too formal."

"But I understand that you have another name," Meg said. "You're also known as the Old Guard."

"Yes, yes, that's correct."

Myra jumped in. "That's your sports blog. I've read several columns. I like to do my homework."

"The dog ate mine," Molly said.

Everybody in the audience but Patty laughed.

"We can always count on Molly," Meg said. "I had the chance to dig a little deeper than just reading your columns, Tim. For our non-sports enthusiasts, it seems that *The Old Guard* refers to your days as a football player."

"Right, right, there I was right in the line being a guard."

Molly scrunched up her nose. "Are guards the big ones?"

"Right you are. We guards had to be big."

"Well, you sure have big arms."

"That might be from the bakery," Timothy said. "There's a lot of stirring and mixing and lifting, even with all of our equipment."

"Bakery?" Myra asked.

"Oh, yes, I own a bakery." Timothy put a finger to his chin. "Dear me, I'm afraid it doesn't give me much time for morning television, though Martin loves your show. He DVRs it faithfully."

"Who's Martin?" Meg asked.

"Oh, he's my partner." Timothy waved toward the camera. "Hi, Martin."

Everybody in the audience laughed, even Patty.

"Well, I'm certainly glad we have a loyal listener in Martin," Myra said, "but I'm sure most of the audience would like to learn more about your interesting ideas for promoting women's sports."

Molly waved to the camera. "Hi, Martin."

Meg jumped in, "Since we've had Myra's introduction and Molly's greetings, I'd like to get right to the heart of your ideas, Tim. I take it from my research that your position about more promotion of women's sports is really about equality."

Timothy looked past Myra to Meg. "That's well stated."

"But money for promotion is only a tool," Myra said. "I think your point, Timothy, is how the power structure regards women's sports."

"Goodness gracious, you both make such cogent comments. I do so hope that encourages your many viewers to also have a look at *The Old Guard.*"

"That's the title of your blog, of course. As we mentioned, the name refers to your past as a football player." Myra winked at the camera. "Isn't so much emphasis on football in college athletics part of the problem?"

"Or, as I understand your position, too little emphasis on women's sports," Meg said. "I know you brought up both softball and volleyball."

"Oh, yes," Timothy said. "I find them both highly entertaining, and I don't mind saying that many of the athletic moves are quite amazing."

"You mean, something you couldn't do as a football player." Myra said.

"Me? Oh, heavens to Betsy, no."

"I think we should be fair," Meg said. "You are a few years past your playing days."

Timothy pinched a lock of gray hair between his fingers. "I'm afraid it's getting to be a few decades."

Molly reached over and touched his arm. "You have really young-looking skin."

He put his hands in his lap. "Thank you."

"You have to tell us your secret," Molly said.

"Well, I do think it's important to moisturize, don't you?" Timothy answered.

Everybody in the audience laughed but Patty.

"It strikes me that your feelings about equality for women in sports may have a more personal angle," Myra said.

"Well, I do wish that all women who deserve credit could receive it."

"I was thinking more of your days in football locker rooms," Myra said as a follow-up.

"Oh my stars, that was so long ago. There's not much to say."

"But you do have very strong feelings about discrimination," Meg said. "It's okay to open up."

"Oh, I hope I have been clear that I believe very fervently in equality."

"No question," Meg said. "I think we would all like to hear more about your personal story. What *was* it like for you to be in a football locker room?"

"Oh, well, my, as I said, there's not really much to tell on that score."

"Don't be shy," Molly said.

"Molly's right," Myra said.

"I am?"

Myra put a hand on Timothy's shoulder. "You're among friends here. You can speak honestly. If you had trouble about gays being in the locker room, I think the world needs to know."

Patty squirmed in her seat.

"Gracious me, why would I have anything against gay people?"

"I know it's hard to be brave," Meg said, "but I think we all know it's not healthy to deflect."

Patty squirmed again. She never should have gotten Timothy into this. It was worse than yesterday. It was going to be the worst day of her life.

"I must say that I've lost your drift," Timothy said to Meg.

"Timothy," Myra said, "we know that gay men have had to hide their sexual orientation in the sports world."

Patty couldn't take it anymore. She sprang out of her seat and hopped onto the stage. She realized she still had pretty good hops left from her basketball playing days. "Stop! He's not the Old Guard. I am."

Two security guards started toward Patty from opposite sides of the stage.

Myra held up a hand. "Wait. Let's hear what this young lady has to say."

A stage manager frantically swung a boom mic in Patty's direction.

"Oh, dear, I've done it again," Timothy muttered.

"You certainly don't look like a football player," Meg said.

"I'm not. I played basketball. I was a guard."

"Are those the little ones?" Molly asked.

"Yes."

Molly nodded. "You do have little feet."

"So, let me get this straight," Myra stared at Patty, "you claim to be the Old Guard."

"I am." Patty's voice cracked. "And who cares about

any old blog, anyway."

Timothy stood. "Now, Patty."

"It's okay," she said. "You don't have to tell them anything about being gay."

Timothy took a step in her direction. "I'm not gay."

"You're not?" Patty said.

"You're not?" "You're not?" "You're not?" Molly, Myra, and Meg said.

"Heavenly days, no. Why do you think I went along with pretending to be the Old Guard?" He kept inching in Patty's direction.

"I thought you wanted to be a good neighbor."

"Gracious sakes alive. Fainting from the cold medicine you gave me, having you put cigarette ashes in my hair, going on the radio with that awful Fred person. Patty, nobody is that good of a neighbor."

Patty started closing the gap between them. "Then why did you help?"

"I wanted to spend the time with you."

"You did?" Patty said.

"You did?" "You did?" "You did?" Molly, Myra, and Meg said.

"Yes," Timothy said.

"But, what about Martin?" Patty asked.

"Right, what about Martin?" Meg echoed.

"He's your partner, isn't he?" Myra asked.

"Who's Martin?" Molly asked.

"He's my partner—in the bakery," Timothy said to Molly, Myra, and Meg.

"So, he's not gay?" Meg asked.

"Oh, well, yes, Martin's gay. He's very open and assured of himself." Timothy turned back toward Patty. "In fact, I don't know why I didn't tell you about Martin's new friend, Bill. He's quite the sportsman. He trains sled dogs up in International Falls. He'd like to race them in the Iditarod one day."

140

"What's an Iditarod?" Molly asked.

"Who cares," Myra and Meg said in unison.

"Doesn't this just prove what my great-grandmother always said. Honesty is the best policy. I should have let you know how much I love spending time with you."

"You do?" Patty said.

"Oh heavens, yes. You're smart and cute and creative, and, well, I'd have to say spunky."

"Ooh," "Ooh," "Ooh," Ooh," Molly, Myra, Meg, and the audience cooed.

Patty smiled. She liked being called spunky. She took another step forward, wrapped her arms around his waist, and buried her face against his chest. His shirt smelled like potpourri. This was going to be the best day of her life.

She just . . . knew it.

ABOUT THE AUTHOR

Tom McKay is a historian and museum consultant who lives in his hometown of Hampton, Illinois. His debut novel, *West Fork*, was published by East Hall Press at Augustana College in 2014. His short novel, *Another Life*, was published by 918studio press in 2014. His short stories have appeared in the *Wapsipinicon Almanac*, *Vermont Ink*, *Downstate Story*, the *Wisconsin River Valley Journal*, the *Book Rack Newsletter*, and the *Out Loud Anthology* series of the Midwest Writing Center.

Made in the USA
Lexington, KY
17 October 2019